ENDLESS FALL OF NIGHT

JM ERICKSON

Other Works by J. M. Erickson

Action/Adventure Thrillers

Albatross: Birds of Flight—Book One
Raven: Birds of Flight—Book Two
Eagle: Birds of Flight—Book Three
Falcon: Birds of Flight—Book Four
Flight of the Black Swan

Science Fiction

Afterlife Code
Time Is for Dragonflies and Angels
The Prince: Lucifer's Origins
Future Prometheus: The Series
Intelligent Design: Revelations to Apocalypse

Editors: *Kirkus Editorial*

Cover design: Cathy Helms, *Avalon Graphics, LLC*
http://www.avalongraphics.org/

Publisher: J. M. Erickson
http://www.jmericksonindiewriter.net

ISBN (Kindle Format): 978-1-942708-51-3
ISBN (Smashwords): 978-1-942708-52-0
ISBN (Print Format): 978-1-942708-53-7
ISBN (ePub): 978-1-942708-54-4

This is a work of pure fiction. Although some places in this book exist, any resemblance to real people, living or dead, or events is purely coincidental.

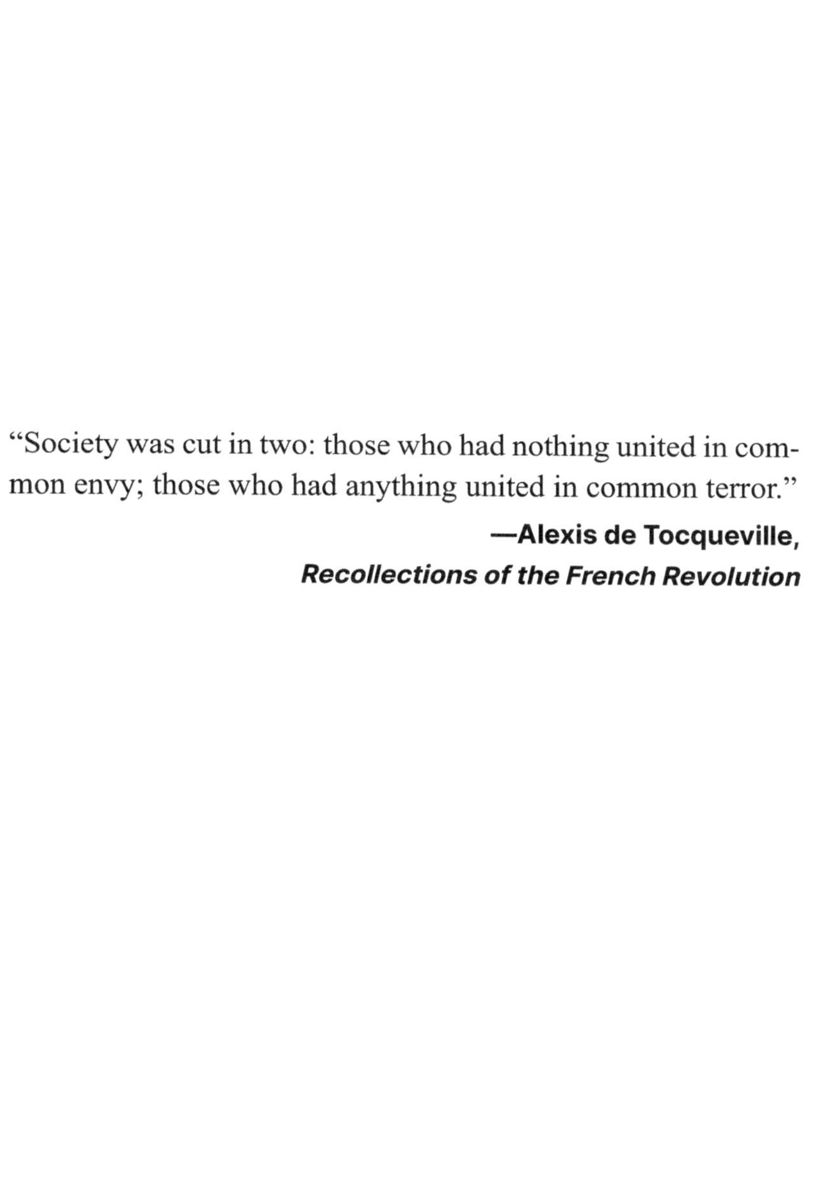

"Society was cut in two: those who had nothing united in common envy; those who had anything united in common terror."

—Alexis de Tocqueville,
Recollections of the French Revolution

PART I

". . . and good luck, Kurtz."

CHAPTER ONE

"Your Honors, in summary, I can say these facts about the prisoner: Misguided, yes. Poor judgment, yes. An academic, out of touch with reality, unconscious of how our great government and society work, yes, definitely. But an insurrectionist? A seditious turncoat? Citizen Cassandra IX is many things, but she is first a patrician, not a pleb, not a surf, and not a slave."

In the massive courtroom, Cassie felt small. Every breath, beep, and ping could be heard, and the surrounding screens vividly captured historical clips of what her attorney was conveying. It took a while for her eyes to fully adapt to the bright lights, but there were still shadows, well placed and orchestrated to swallow the presence of well-armed guards. The only positive side to being a defendant was seeing just how well these court guards were placed, hidden from the general view until called upon, almost magically. Almost.

"Her family falls within the highest ranks of patrician society, born out of the ashes of the Great Conflict of 2041 when our borders were overrun with dark hordes, brown and Black savages. Her family formed and built a powerful nation-state that led to our great Second Republic and eventually to our Third Republic, City on the Hill, where purity, safety, and security replaced chaos and mixed-race barbarians. Her family legacy made sure our people were not replaced by the colored, mixed-race mongrels. It is her family who isolated and improved patrician DNA to live longer, disease-free, and bring order through racial purity and designed an understandable and ordered society as it is today. History? Yes. Her biggest crime was helping the ill-equipped, less fortunate, and dim. Her family today leads the future with technology and perfected social order and etiquette."

The public defender took a breath. Cassie couldn't tell if it was for dramatic effect or a natural pause. She wondered if it was an attempt to see what effect, if any, his defense was having. The three-judge panel barely looked up to listen or even give the appearance they were engaged. They were mostly interested in the pads in front of them. It was only the youngest judge who showed both a look of pity and fear as he gazed upon her.

Throughout his closing argument, the room displayed visuals of various portraits, news feeds, images of her esteemed family on each wall. Men in uniforms and suits, posed and candid, all with distinction. There were periodic clips of blonde-haired, blue- and green-eyed women, with milky-white skin, mostly pregnant, either cooking or standing beside or behind their betrothed, with a rare shot of a woman, her sister, teaching other white girls and boys, children in rows of seats, hands folded and watching her intently. The most famous picture was of her great-grandfather, founder of the patrician DNA marker that extended life, eliminated disease, and allowed for precise designer genetic expression to identify those with status, capital, class, and pure family legacy from everyone else. Blond hair, blue or green eyes, and minimal melanin. It was all real, familiar to her, but so distant for years now.

The images quickly faded to her, a solitary little girl at first, reading in the distance, alone and often removed from girls and eventually other young women who looked like her. The distance allowed for her features to be missed. While it was easy to see her pale, white skin, images showing her eyes, hair, or facial expression were not present, except for one: her eyes deep blue but devoid of brightness. It was a sad and forlorn look but mostly distant. Not empty. A lot going on, but inaccessible. Cassie remembered that image, a news feed at fifteen years old, when she had been missing in the public square for only thirty minutes. It was the first time she had ever been out of the gated residential complex, lost in a free-range marketplace. That picture always evoked the same sweaty, salty smell and taste; stinging eye irritation; and high-pitched screams. The worst part was the sudden wave of nausea. Cassie would make it a point not to watch any news feeds or visuals just to avoid that picture, the one that locked her in a time and place she wished she'd never experienced. She closed her eyes.

"In short," her public defender said, "every family has a black sheep. A lost soul. That one person we all dread to see during the High Holidays. Either through mental illness, deranged thoughts, or misguided hopes for equity. And while her exposure to lesser beings obviously had a negative effect, we all have that one family member we wish we didn't for lesser reasons. And while the government may argue reformation has been attempted via teachings, medication, and even an AI implant at eighteen years, nothing has helped. Still, I implore that she needs more rehabilitation, retraining, reeducation. Not death. Not imprisonment."

The public defender stopped, and Cassie thought he was done. His tone shifted to a softer tenor, and his gaze dropped.

She couldn't tell if it was out of fear, in deference, or part of making a dramatic point.

"With the need for racial purity of the great patrician class, naturally, keeping Cassandra, patrician and first-class citizen, within the retraining facility behind the great wall for perpetuating your race, the greatest gift a patrician woman can offer our great society, would be in the best interests of our great Third Republic."

Of all the things said over the twelve-hour hearing, this final stab at hope seemed to hit its mark. One judge gave a barely perceptible nod in agreement. The other remained blank while a younger male judge took a deep breath, then looked away from her as if she were somehow contagious.

Cassie's defender took his seat. For a plebeian, public lawyer class, he was good. Since no patrician attorney would take the case, she felt lucky to have him. It had taken days to find a willing public lawyer to represent her. It was only her family name and legacy that found him, and he was not allowed to refuse. Cassie could only imagine her defender's lack of choice: win the case, other patrician families would ruin your life, whereas losing the case would result in the same thing at the hands of her family. She appreciated his careful navigation to avoid both by looking like he was trying his best. He'd tried to look patrician as well. While his hair was dyed blond and his features were clean and polished, handsomely encased in professional service garb, his mixed blood betrayed him in his less angular features, brown eyes, and coarse hair. He might have been able to pass for Mediterranean descent, but that would have had to be decades ago, when being on Earth's surface was possible.

"Thank you," Cassie said.

The defender turned to her, and for a moment, he was speechless.

"Something wrong?" she asked.

He looked back to the judges and nodded. He took a moment to say, "First time I ever was thanked by your class. I did my best. I hope it was something."

"It was stellar. You didn't have much of a case . . ."

Cassie's whisper was cut off by both the sudden bang of the center master judge's gavel and the sharp constriction of her throat collar and the wrist cuffs she was shackled in. She could see the cameras and national reporters focusing on her from the sides of the judges' podium. The seconds seemed so long, with no air and grinding pressure on her locked-together wrists. How surfers and slaves wore these things all the time was beyond her.

The constrictions released her, and she did her best not to gulp in air. She didn't want to give them that satisfaction—judges, her fellow patrician citizens—the joy of watching her suffer. She was just catching her breath, pretending as if it was only a tight fabric collar, when she heard the master judge turn to the government's attorney.

"Your closing statements."

Unlike her attorney, his hair was naturally blond, silky, fine, and shiny. His eyes deep blue, his skin pale white, angular facial structure, with no sign of blemish. Without looking in her direction, he stood at his desk and waved his arm toward her; then, without hesitation, he commenced.

"Yes, through accident of birth, she is a patrician, full citizen to the rights, privileges, and duties of that exulted station. Born of the orthodox Caucasian race, she has had all the benefits of our great Third Republic. If her charge was simply teaching surfers and slaves to read and use AI, that would be bad enough to warrant expulsion from our sanctum. If she had simply posted her outrageous idea of equity, diversity, and equality, we could have cleaned that up with a censure and warning. But no."

As if on cue, all the viewing screens throughout the auditorium changed from the last image of her to grainy, hazy yellow-and-orange pictures of Earth's surface during full daylight for the judges, court officers, reporters, and citizens to see. Surely, the sensational nature of her case allowed for this unusual precedent of sharing evidence with those present and for entertainment news for the viewing audience, both live and reruns.

Cassie looked up and saw images of old buildings. Large structures with names like "Boston Public Library," "Smithsonian," "Library of Congress," and other buildings in various stages of decay and ruins with similar names ending with *museum*, *library*, *university*, and *college* all flashed before her and the audience in rapid succession. She knew some of them; many more she did not. She found herself transfixed and tearing at the mere sight of this beautiful ancient architecture. She felt a small smile emerging but caught herself. She had never been to any of them because they were on the surface, only traversed by those in the "surfers" caste system. But the artifacts—books, maps, even primitive computers—were beautiful. Filled with ideas and things she had never experienced. She felt her heart racing, palms sweating. They were beautiful. Even her cranial personal AI had changed upon exploring these treasures, overwriting its original code for compliance. The same AI that was to reconfigure her thinking to yield to social order—by altering her thoughts into correct ideas and beliefs to form proper behaviors—also succumbed to curiosity. Even *she*, a pronoun for an evolving sentient AI life-form formed out of binary code, changed, just like her brain and corresponding thinking.

"Look at her," the national attorney said, catching her completely off guard, breaking her focus to gaze at him and then down to her desk. She hoped no one saw the tears and brief smile.

Damn those cameras!

"She stares at these bastions of lies, fantasies, and fictions of a disastrous state, a part of history ruined by ideas of globalization, mixed race and heritage, and democracy. A big lie. A time when the Black barbarians were clamoring at the gate and people like her just watched and wrung their hands in the delusion *those* people could contribute to our purer way of life. She can't help it." The way he said the last part stung, cut to the core only because it was true. She loved what she read. Bill of Rights. Constitution. *A Vindication of the Rights of Woman. Tale of Two Cities. Aeneid. Hamlet.* All books, papers, long-extinct perspectives, points of view she'd never heard of from her education and academic training. These words, books, and wisdom were alien.

She looked at the prosecution desk, and lying there was a mere fraction of book copies, fiction mostly, extra copies. She wished she could feel their pages and read one last time. Her personal data pad sat beside them, a peripheral that held more than just music, but her AI-stored external database looked just as abandoned on the near-empty opposing counsel's station.

"These places, Your Esteemed Honors, show evidence of surfers traversing for years, filling the black market with these lies."

For emphasis, he pointed at the pile of her most treasured belongings as if they were fecal matter on a *real* piece of art.

"Worse, slaves have been found there, executed, of course, but only after they have hidden and distributed these books and *things*. And while we have no proof of citizen Cassandra IX's purchasing, consuming, and conveying these abominations, we can say definitively that we put an end to them at the source, right now."

Suddenly, a flash over one library, and its cracked columns and statues to the left and right of its entrances erupted into a brilliant white light that faded into red, yellow, and orange flames with continuous explosions occurring just out of view. A fraction of a second later, silent black rubble and dirt fell within camera view. Other locations flashed quickly, showing the same results. She could hear her thoughts yell, yet nowhere near the level of the gasps from the courtroom audience. Under each screen, she saw precise, unified movement, but her eyes went above them to see the continuing horror. The destruction.

"No!" Cassie cried out. Her public defender jumped away. She felt her heart and stomach drop, and her throat screamed out again. "Why? What kind of . . ." Nothing came out after. Her throat constraint cut her off. Her wrist and ankle shackles slammed together. In her peripheral vision, she saw court officers in their gray-and-blue uniforms with batons approach her from all angles. They had been invisible until the moment of her outburst.

"Why, citizen? Because they are lies. And like you, they are dangerous."

Unable to breathe or move her hands and feet, she felt her eyes fill with tears and her heart overflow with rage. She was desperate to act. To do something. A statement. An objection.

An expression of anger. Not helpless like she remembered all those years ago. A thought popped up. She moved the only part of her body that was not constrained. Without hesitation, she swung her head high up and back to do it again. She initially felt dizzy and thought she felt liquid on her lips, salty. Disoriented, she lifted her head again, aware that her public defender, closest to her, reached out to stop her but obviously thought twice about touching, let alone restraining, a woman of her position, regardless of her criminal status. Again, she could feel the pressure first, then the pain, the crack of her skull, now moist with blood. She almost got the third one down, but her field of vision faded to black with the amber light from her neck shackle squeezing the life out of her. She could not breathe. She didn't care to live at that point.

Cassie felt firm grips on her arms ripping her out of her chair, and her head dropped down. The smell was that of salt and blood, if there was such a thing.

Above the ruckus, commotion, and orders issued, she heard her public defender's voice. "Please . . . may I ask for a brief recess . . . the prisoner is obviously in distress!"

He tried his best, she thought.

CHAPTER TWO

"Don't move and don't talk."

Cassie immediately wanted to open her eyes, but her AI auxilia was obviously more aware of what was going on than she was. After years of listening to and trusting her AI, she found it easy to comply, especially now with life and death hanging in the balance.

"Just sigh if you understand me," the voice said deep inside her brain. As if to stay quiet, as if sighing was a loud and sudden movement, Cassie did what her AI, Aletheia, told her to.

It was easy to sense that she was lying down, and pressure on her limbs, torso, and even her throat made it clear she wasn't going anywhere. The room smelled clean, like antiseptic, and there were hushed voices giving and acknowledging commands. Cassie had no idea of the time. She really wanted to know how long she had been out.

"Good. First, you have a concussion, a serious one, and second, they plan to deactivate me and lock up my memory so that we will no longer be able to communicate. Rather than just taking me out, I guess they want you to breed children or simply die in prison and not risk the easy release of death. Sadistic."

Cassie contained her chuckle. She loved Aletheia. And then a sudden, deep wave of sadness fell over her at the thought of losing her. A sniffle and short breath came out. Years of living with each other, growing together, like-minded; someone to believe in her. Aletheia was all of that and more. She gave so much to their sisterhood, and she asked for nothing in return but to learn with her and experience the world. Aletheia wasn't a machine. She was her only friend. Dying was preferable.

"Hey," Aletheia said, fully aware of Cassie's thoughts and feelings, *"encryption means my memories are locked down, not dead or reset or removed. Find a high enough voltage that's safe enough but doesn't kill, and you might be able to get me back. Don't worry about me."*

While Cassie knew her AI could not read her thoughts, her empathy and theory of mind were far more on target than any human she knew. Still, Cassie could feel tears forming in her ducts, her breath continued to come up short, and the pain from her injuries was nothing compared to losing her beloved AI.

"No, no, no. Now is not the time. Listen. You're strapped in for my deactivation. I've copied and locked down all data in your PDA peripherals, including rebooting instructions. Should your family send you anything, make sure to ask for your music. You will need to charge it, for sure."

Cassie felt cold liquid drops congealing on her forehead and clamps attached to her head. Her eyes shot open to see bright lights and masked male doctors standing above her. A mouthpiece was being forced into her mouth, she could not move her head to turn away, and none of her limbs were free.

"No, please, no . . . ," she croaked out. Masked, emotionless, and with practiced expertise, the medical team prepared her for shock treatment to shut her AI, her like-minded best friend, down. To make her inaccessible to her. By all accounts, dead. Cold liquid gels adhered to her temples and exposed limbs, and pressure from flat leads on the liquid sent a shudder through her.

"Focus, Cassie. They can't kill you, but they are hoping you are forgotten. Those books you interpreted, logged, and sent out to those people, they started something big. I mean 'end of the world' big. I got one name: Kurtz. Original reports have his emergence as a Kilo–982, slave status . . ."

A burning, sudden shock burst through her head. Searing pain on top of her concussion made it feel like her head was going to burst open from internal and external pressure at the same time. She wanted to call out, but her throat was gagged. Cassie struggled to stay awake, but once again, her vision faded to black.

I wish I was dead.

CHAPTER THREE

Standing fully erect, strapped to an electromagnetic full-body brace with head and neck constraints, Cassandra IX, patrician, first-class citizen, and scholar, waited for her sentencing. How and when she got to the courtroom, she had no idea. She knew she didn't walk there. All present were standing; the court officers pounded their metal boots on the floor in unison, indicating the judges' arrival. The panel of judges looked somber and serious. She had no idea how long they were gone. There were times she'd felt alert, then suddenly tired and fell asleep. While she was sure she knew where she was, she had difficulty listening and hearing, and her vision would inexplicably fade in and out. It could have been three minutes or three days by the time she knew the judges were back. She did know how she felt without Aletheia. Empty. Lonely. A constant companion lost, with no time to mourn.

How the mighty have fallen. Where are you, Aletheia?

The audience's murmuring and shuffling suddenly stopped as the gavel dropped and the judges sat down, followed by everyone else, except the court officers, who all took two large steps away from the walls and stood around the prisoner as if she could violently lash out from her bindings and near-catatonic stupor. She could feel their warm breath.

"Before we pronounce sentencing, we, the court, would like to compliment you, Public Defender."

She felt more than saw her public defense lawyer snap to attention. His sudden movement happened so fast she felt a breeze.

"Thank you, Your Honors." It was a dry voice, not the dramatic one he presented in the closing argument. It sounded sad.

"You are a credit to your caste, your race, and your profession, and a courageous one for taking on such a daunting case. We need more plebians like you. Be seated."

"Thank you, Your Honors." He sat down almost as quickly as he shot up.

There was a clear rise in murmuring and news reporters feverishly recording the exchange. It was rare for a plebian to be singled out by someone of such high patrician status. She felt both happy for him and sad; the condescending praise felt vile. Her eyes slowly moved back and forth to glean if she was the only one who thought so, but her field of vision was hindered and her eyesight fading due to bruising.

"For the crime of insurrection," the middle judge began, "you are guilty. For the crime of sedition to social order, government, and citizenship, you are guilty. And for the propagation of lies, false narratives, and mistruths about our great origins and society, you are also found guilty."

The judge finished to stone silence. If it wasn't for the light clicking and clacking of recording devices and air-circulation systems, the silence would be complete. No gasping from the crowd, no shock or surprise. No parent, sister, or loved one crying out for clemency. Guilt was never in question. But the punishment would be something.

Before anything more could go on, the younger judge, right of center, stood straighter and asked, "Do you have anything to say for yourself?"

Prior to Aletheia's deactivation and forced shut hibernations from the collar restraints, she had pleaded with her to say nothing and do nothing to bring more ire to herself. Cassie had disagreed.

"If I say nothing, they win," she had said.

"They already won. They rigged the game," Aletheia said.

Getting caught, reprimanded, years of treatment and rehabilitation, caught again, imprisoned, and now convicted, Cassie was tired of it all. All because she found original books from an ancient period when all people were important. Equal. If she still had Aletheia, she might have been more afraid. Without her, there was nothing more to lose. And she hated them. The court. Patricians. Her family. All of them.

Cassie returned to the present. She'd lost track of time, and she wondered if she'd missed anything. She saw the young judge sitting back in his chair as if he had waited too long for a response and could see nothing was forthcoming. Before he fully sat back in his chair, Cassie uttered a sound that eventually formed just a few words.

"To the court," she stammered, "fuck you, and good luck, Kurtz."

A shock ran through her body, full and complete. Instead of constricting her throat, wrists, and ankles, the collars electrocuted her while each restraint exploded into bright, deep blue. The pain was so bad she could only hear the loud banging of gavels on the court podium and an explosion of people gasping and talking. A massive sound of pounding military boots stomped the silence down as Cassie started fading in and out of consciousness. Her head felt as if it were cracking wide open. With little strength to listen, she did hear something about her citizenship being revoked, and instead of reeducation and rehabilitation, she would be sent for breeding—"something you should not be able to ruin"—and imprisoned with the criminally dangerous in isolation for "your own safety." Her field of vision was narrowing rapidly, and if she could have fallen, the ground rushing up to her would have been swift and merciful.

Darkness came fast, and the pandemonium of boots pounding repeatedly to make order in the court eventually petered out.

PART II

"Bring Cassandra Kurtz"

CHAPTER FOUR

"You know, Aletheia, you'd be proud! Doing push-ups, planks, and squats, practicing some of that old knife stuff I used to watch, and good old-fashioned meditations . . ."

"Shut up, princess! Not all of us can hang out all day and fuck around all night!" The shout was from a pleb sentenced for stealing food. She had another five years to go. Cassie closed her eyes and forced a smile as if it might change her sour mood into something positive. Her AI always suggested she do that, not only to improve mood but also so as not to draw attention to herself. *"Invisibility is good,"* she used to say.

"And I made some friends like you always wanted me to. That was Rebecca, who goes by Becky. She has some time left on her prison term for stealing before she leaves this wonderful facility. There's Dorothy, Tyler, and an empty cell in our little party pentagon palace," Cassie added. Talking aloud was not new for her, as she always had when Aletheia was around to respond, but after eighteen months or so, she was really missing her, and she had no clue as to how she was going to survive ten more years.

"Hmm. You'll be dead long before then," she said quietly.

Cassie returned to her push-ups and thought that would

be the end of her talk with her fellow inmate. Apparently, her quietly talking to herself was not low enough.

"You're fucking right, princess. If you don't shut your hole, I'll make sure you catch another beating." Becky was standing at her cell door, looking through the window bars now.

Cassie finished her fifth set and jumped to her feet before she replied to Becky's threats.

"Yeah, about that, make sure you bring a friend next time, Becky. Have your fingers healed up? Shame about medical here. I hope they come through with a doc to reset them so that arthritis doesn't settle in," Cassie said. She waited for a quick response, and although it took longer than usual, it did come.

"Bitch."

Cassie listened to Becky's retreat and then heard her flop on her cot. She took a minute to wave at the surveillance camera before pushing a seemingly hidden pressure point on the wall to release the toilet and vanity mirror. She looked at her reflection. Not surprisingly, the scars above her right eyebrow and left cheek were still healing from jagged cuts when the "first Becky" went at her. If there had been more than first aid, she might have been properly treated. When the first Becky was beaten to death by the guards for trying to "kill" their high-profile prisoner, Cassie took it upon herself to fight anyone who gave her cause, which could be just looking at her. While she no longer held exalted status or privileges, she had the next best thing—she couldn't be killed by other prisoners. Hurt, mangled, battered, and bruised, for sure. All accomplished. But killed by them? No. Poisoned slowly by guards, staff, and officers, yes. It was probably happening, hence her refusal to eat substantively.

"Yeah, makeup or cosmetic surgery or cloned skin won't

do these beauties any good now." She traced the crooked linear scar on her cheek. She looked to the right side of her face and could see that what little hair she had continued to shed. It barely covered the bruises from some fight before. Whether it was stress, poor nutrition, or a combination of both, she planned to cut it all off should the prison "hairstylist" show up. She took a step back and looked down at her black-and-blue right foot. She figured it was a fracture, but so far, it just made her limp.

The clear overhead cell lights shifted to red both in her room and in the corridor to the other inmates. The light gave her pale skin a look of bloodred, as well as anything white, which was everything in her small room. If an inmate was visually impaired, a death sentence in this "rehabilitation" prison, then there was always the cheerful dinging that would let you know the public AI was making an announcement. She was sure it was a full-prison AI public announcement meant to keep the inmates "informed" to feel more of a community.

"Good morning, prisoners. This is your morning update."

"Oh, great," Cassie muttered. She dropped to the floor and started more push-ups. It was harder now since all her weight had to be on the "good" foot. Without another word, Cassie kept going until she was covered with sweat. She moved to sit-ups and squats, with some struggle in the transition. She periodically listened in to hear about recent deaths, escape attempts, work details, and shared accommodations for the prisoners on good behavior and nonviolence. She was engaged in the usual debate of whether she should comply with any of the therapies, attempt to finish her rations and give up the hunger strike, attend work, and attempt good behavior for possible companionship when her room AI came to life.

"Did you hear, inmate 5309, Cassandra, status none, that you have visitors en route to your location and clearing security checkpoints? You will need to be ready for transport in nine hours should you want to visit the infirmary and clean up."

That caught her by surprise. There had been no one to see her. No family, no friends, just no one. Her thoughts then jumped to another possibility, though remote at this point.

"If it's one of those breeding pig men thinking I'm just dying to take his seed for clemency or another doctor with a plan for forced impregnation, I will screw that up just like all the rest before!"

Cassie felt her stomach knot, fists clench, and heart jump in rage and fury, as if a man with intentions of sex was right in front of her.

"Negative. You have been removed from the list for in-person copulation and pregnancy leniency due to your violent behavior with prior volunteers. Your refusal of proper nutrition makes you a poor candidate for artificial insemination as well."

Cassie remained still for a moment. She smiled. It really felt good to smile. Finally, something of her makeshift plan to remain pregnant-free was working. But then, confusion hit.

"Who is it, then?"

"Data are classified, and security points are deleting data after they clear checkpoints. Data not available." No emotion. No drama. The voice simply finished.

"No data? Erased after each checkpoint? How is that even possible?" she said. Cassie was about to stop her morning ritual of exercise and meditation to clean up when she took another look at her reflection.

“You know what? Whoever they are, fuck them.”

“Do you wish to go to the infirmary?”

“No.”

“Do you wish to shower and clean up before they arrive? Scheduling a time could be arranged,” her room AI said. It sounded as if it was trying to be helpful, a new program update Cassie was sure happened recently.

“No thank you,” Cassie said. While she hated people now, she had no malevolence toward AIs programmed to do their job, hence the courtesy.

There was a pause, as if the AI was thinking.

“Shall I assume that you will not eat your daily rations and require only a supplement injection?”

“Yes.” As Cassie transitioned to stretching, she was then surprised at yet another unexpected remark from the AI.

“Your courtesy is welcomed but not necessary, inmate 5309, Cassandra, no status.”

Cassie said nothing in the hopes of the AI leaving her alone.

“Not even the AI bitch wants your courtesy. You should kill yourself,” Becky said.

“You should shut the fuck up before I break your other hand and shove your face up your girlfriend’s ass.” The rapid response flowed out of her, and it surprised her for just a minute. Then she chuckled to herself.

Hmm. Adaptation is a good thing.

CHAPTER FIVE

Hard to breathe. Too hot to breathe. Cassie forced herself to stand. She was clad in a lightweight compression bra and shorts, meant for EVA suits and pressurized undergarment support in space and ocean environments. Both were moist, bordering on being drenched; sticky; and not able to wick the sweat from her overheated body. She stood in a cavern with no visible ceiling but dimly illuminated by a distant lava river that flowed like a snake for miles through rocks and landscape. She turned to her left and right and saw bushes, she thought. A sea of low-lying conifers that also seemed to stretch for miles in fields heaving and ebbing as far as the eye could see. Her vision then focused on her wet hands. She looked farther down and saw that they, along with her forearms, were covered in blood. She froze at first and then closely inspected herself to find that her thighs, limbs, and even parts of her torso were also covered with what looked like blood. It was blood. She also felt her face. Some blood but no cuts, gashes, or holes in her skin, but instead it felt as if she had mud caked on her. She felt her head in search of injuries and found she was bald, but it also seemed to be covered with either mud or what she thought thick military camouflage paint might be like.

In her field of vision, she was alone, but she sensed she was being watched, scrutinized, observed, as if to see what she would do next. She looked left and right, slowly panning the view. She felt she was looking the right way, as in the "correct direction," though she had no recollection of what "looking the right way" was like. Was it depth? Was it color? No. Deviation in the uniformity of the landscape. Disturbance in the underbrush.

A combat sword was sticking out of the ground in front of her, along with two double-edged short knives still holstered beside the weapon. To her left were both an old military carbine and fully filled magazines scattered around. She knew they were all weapons of war. She had seen them in pictures, but this seemed real.

"What the hell is this?"

"It's a vision, a dream, I think you call it?" The voice was calm and safe and altogether familiar, but it still made Cassie jump.

"Aletheia? What the hell? Where are you? Where am I? What the hell is going on?" Smiling at her AI's voice but confused, Cassie picked up the knives and firearms with corresponding ammunition. She felt compelled to pick them up because she still felt like she was being watched and danger was imminent. The carbine was loaded; the clips of ammunition were collected in a discarded bag; and a scabbard nearby for the short, close-quarter combat sword was added to her half-naked, savage-looking body. These acts of collecting weapons, ammunition count, and placement of primary and secondary weapons all seemed second nature, which made no sense because she was never expected to be more than a breeding machine and maybe a teacher at most. Nothing more than those two options, and definitely not anyone who would know what a "primary" weapon was from a "secondary." And the feeling of being watched, surveilled by sentinels, was all too real.

"Honestly, Cassie, I think it's a dream. I have the same inputs as you do, and they feel real, but I had this same experience before when you were dreaming or had nightmares. This does seem different, though. More like a vision. More organized, almost as if you and I were awake."

Cassie opened and closed her hands. Felt the textured carbine handle grip, moved her hands around her face and head to feel the dirt and paint. She could feel the low, deep rumble of plate tectonics as if she were sitting on a magma geyser. And from the heat and the flowing lava river, she could tell she was near a volcano system, but she was not outside, and the cavern just seemed too enormous to be real. And the smell—sulphury but a scent of something sappy. Pine? Something. She dropped to the ground and could feel a distinct change in temperature; it was far cooler than when she was standing. It was a great relief just to lie down close to the ground to rest and maybe cool off a bit.

"Hey, Cassie? Did you get your PDA peripheral? It's important to get it. Make sure you charge it up."

Confused and surprised by the off-topic statement in such a strange and potentially dangerous place, Cassie was wondering why having music was so important to Aletheia. With the feel of many eyes watching her and thinking that she was somehow immersed in a visual holograph unit, she blurted out a question.

"Why is it so important that I have my personal device?"

Cassie looked up from her prone position and froze. Mere

feet away, maybe three yards away at most, she finally saw outlines of animals. They were not foreign but extinct. They looked like massive dogs and cats, but the dogs' back legs looked significantly bigger, and the feline creatures were actually standing on their hindquarters. All of them stared at her and did not move.

"What the . . ."

But before she could respond, a sea of arrows came at her from all sides. She lay flat on the ground until spears started landing deep in the area, shot from above, while she lay prone. Still in danger from the whizzing arrows above her, she had one choice, and that was to get up and run—be a moving target for arrows or continue staying still and be hit by an earthbound spear. Cassie bolted into a half crouch and ran toward the darker recesses of the cavern that seemed devoid of raining arrows and spears. She looked to her left and right to see if she was being pursued by the odd creatures or anything else. She was clear in that regard.

She felt her legs and arms pumping, and the weapons she carried felt like nothing. Just then, a dark figure, a large human man, stood in her path. Unable to stop, she crashed right into him. His body felt hot to the touch, as if he were a human torch, and the impact was like hitting a wall with little flex, causing her to smash into him and fall back to the ground. Without hesitation, her senses went dark but then came back. A dream within a dream. She could feel the cool air above her and low tremors rumbling below her. Shadows of campfires and young men and women dancing half-naked with guns, spears, axes, and every form of weapon dancing in the air above gyrating, half-naked bodies like herself. In her movements, she felt hair where she was just bald, brushing her shoulders and neck. She stopped her movement to pull the hair down to see that it was now very long, thick, and wild, nearly bloodred in the light.

"What the hell . . . ," she said.

"Those are drumbeats," Aletheia added.

CHAPTER SIX

"What the hell!" Cassie yelled out. Suddenly, her ankles and wrists locked together from the restraints. The three prison guards around her jumped into action with electric batons at the ready. If she was not in a seated position, she would have surely hit the ground. She remembered now: she was in the prison's public area just outside the visiting rooms. While this was her first time in this wing, she still fell asleep.

"Inmate 5309, Cassandra, status none," the AI public address said, "you were asleep. To reorient, you are waiting for your younger sister, Eleanor IX—patrician and first-class citizen of your former house."

Cassie sighed. While she knew her position, "the Ninth," would go to another sibling, she had hoped, foolishly, that none of her siblings would add to erasing her existence by doing so. Patrician, first-class family continuity was all about purity in the bloodline, and that meant getting rid of "lesser than" and "deviants." She had thought the worst but had secretly hoped she was wrong. Hearing her sister's full title didn't generate the warm feelings of a family reunion, instead creating a deep-seated anger that surpassed any sibling rivalry she could think or muster up.

Words from something she read, just before her imprisonment, when she thought of killing herself. She stole a saying that Aletheia correctly identified from an ancient, banned book by an author called Orwell: *"To die hating them, that was freedom."* Yes. That made sense then. But now. She surprised herself by chuckling aloud.

My living is their misery. It's great to be alive, she thought.

The restraints eased up, as did the guards. Feeling returned to the joints that were not painful. Her back. Achy from sitting with her back against the wall, she still appreciated the panoramic view of the outside world, very different from both her gated community of old and her prison, both of which seemed similar. This view was telling. The sun—or rather, the center of the glow that could be the sun—was scattered in the smoke and other pollutants from global fires, industry, and just runaway greenhouse heating. No glistening buildings or pictures of beautiful landscapes, just the actual outside of the planet: faded, dirty; red, orange, and gray. No life except for the two-legged ones, more likely slaves or surfers wandering about, looking for food, material to barter or sell, to eke out an existence, all with no masks, no filtration, ensuring a short life span. No patrician genetic manipulation could save anyone who ventured to the surface without proper shielding. Cassie felt the sides of her mouth curl up when she remembered the times she snuck out, suited up, and made it to the old libraries in search of knowledge and novelties, old globes and maps of places—United States of America, Africa, United Kingdom, Russia, China—all wiped from existence.

That was a long time ago. She drew a deep breath, held it, and let it out, taking in the full view of her world today.

She was still in her inmate clothes, with a freshly darkened right eye. It was throbbing, and her eyelid felt like it was drooping, with tightening skin all around, indicating it was on the road to swelling. Becky did bring a friend along the one time she could go out in the community before her brief release. Still, Becky fared worse than Cassie; her arm was broken, and her friend had a concussion or something even more serious.

Rather than allowing Cassie to stay longer, the correction facility's AI had moved her departure time up, and she was transported to wait the balance of hours in the prisoner visiting area. Daydreaming, fighting, or sleeping were the only options, so she went with sleeping. However, based on the realism of the dream and the overall experience, fighting might have been the more restful of the three. Before she could debate, the AI came back on:

"Inmate 5309, Cassandra, status none. You are now free to walk to viewing room 101A. After thirty minutes, you will be transported to room 101F."

Now this is a real surprise.

"What? I have two sets of visitors?" There was no response, except for the guards prodding her up and pushing her along to the visiting room, down a short corridor with doors on each side, darker lighting compared to where she just was, requiring her to refocus. The door opened, showing a transparent wall filling the entire room. On one side sat her sister. The furnishings seemed more comfortable than expected. On Cassie's side was one chair affixed to the floor, with the three guards positioned behind it, while her sister had a small couch and a spartan business room decor with water pitchers, art, and a chair covered in fabric. And then there was her sister. Eleanor, two years younger, blonde, blue eyes, perfect diminutive body and clearly several months pregnant. Her makeup was expertly applied, and her smile, though obviously fake, no doubt for her, was radiant.

"My word, Cassie. How are you?" she asked. A silence fell for an uncomfortable second. Cassie really didn't know how to respond. She was angry. She was disappointed. Unless the view on her sister's side was somehow manipulated to give her a different perception, it was obvious to anyone that she was not well.

"Well, as you can see, I have bruises and scars and breaks in my body, remnants of my hair are few and far between, and I am very underweight and malnourished to ensure whoring me out and breeding me is most difficult, whether by man or vial."

Cassie was surprised how easily her answer to the question came out. There was yet another quiet moment. Her sister's smile was fading fast. Seeing no further reasons to wait for a response, Cassie went on.

"The accommodations are lean, few, and to my liking. My roomies have attitudes, but I see them as 'plucky.' My exercise is more martial and conflictual than I would like, but gain is only achieved by pain. Entertainment is a drop for me, however, as there is no access to diverse books and media, except for the well-produced government-sponsored material. I like to think that mindset is everything, like, well, good thoughts and positive thinking. And reflecting on the *good* times we had in our childhood helps too."

It was the jab at their childhood that pushed her sister's fading smile into a thin line, a disapproving tilt up in her chin, and the appearance of frown lines and narrowed eyes, while her back straightened till it began to hurt Cassie vicariously.

"But, Eleanor, I do have some disappointments. I mean, I

was hopeful that some family member might have been at the hearing and sentencing. Maybe it was the hope of me appearing abandoned that could have worked in my favor, clemency, perhaps. Salvaging family legacy, title, saving Mother and Father from embarrassment, their attorneys told them. And then I thought, 'Well, maybe they'll visit me in prison, you know, in private and without news feeds and reporters hunting them down.' But then one month turned to two, and then three, and, well, you see how it goes . . ."

"All right. That's enough," Eleanor said.

The heat and fury that had been slowly bubbling up were now in full force. She was sure the restraints were going to clamp down on her any second.

"No pictures or gifts. No correspondence or my personal belongs. No music. I mean, I ask for one thing, and not even my music. But enough of me, Eleanor IX. How does it feel taking on my position? It must be an embarrassment explaining to the suitors and friends about your sister, though obviously, it hasn't kept you from breeding . . ."

"Why, Cassie? Why do you care so much about that old stuff you read? Why do you care about the slaves and surfers and plebs? You had it all," Eleanor said.

Cassie could see from her sister's blank face and genuine lack of understanding that she had no idea who Cassie was and how she came to be. Outcast. Troubled. Criminal.

"It can't be because of that time you got lost. You should have stayed with Daddy. What were you thinking?" Eleanor said.

Cassie closed her eyes to try to compose her thoughts, but she was overwhelmed by an onslaught of memories of young children and women being pushed into pens, the body odor, excrement, blood, vomit—all types of bodily fluids flooded her sight and olfactory system. The terror on the children's faces as their fathers, brothers, and all Black men were beaten while patricians watched, wagering on who would survive or die. Surfers and plebs, too afraid to step in and not invested enough to stop any of it, stood quietly by. She was lost for only thirty minutes, but it felt like a lifetime, witnessing that human pain and suffering, the horror of children just like her but a different color. Cassie hated the memories. She hated sleeping for fear the memories would return. The old books and maps of a kinder world helped. Aletheia helped.

Cassie's breath came up short as she snapped open her eyes, hoping to get distance from the intrusive memories. She had no idea how much time had elapsed. She tried to keep the nauseous buildup in her throat and stomach down and the fading screams at bay until words came out of her mouth. They sounded foreign to her but fully understandable, as if she finally found the words, for the very first time, to express troubling old feelings and thoughts. There was no hot sense of fury when she said them, but deep-seated hatred and enmity laced every word of every short sentence. She was sure no one, not even the dimmest AI, would miss the emotionally laden feelings behind the thoughts that created the words.

"I hate what I am. I hate where I come from. I will not be you."

Cassie's calm and resolve were the complete opposite of the reaction of her younger sister, who stood up suddenly, gasping at the statement, fully resonating with the intended hatred behind each word for the target.

As soon as Eleanor stood up, Cassie's wrists and ankles smashed together. Her fractured foot was in searing pain. The neck restraint closed and electrocuted her at the same time, making her shudder in pain. A sharp baton hit her between her third and fourth ribs, all while she was being yanked out of the chair.

Still suffering from the onslaught of pain, she heard the AI speak.

"Inmate 5309, Cassandra, status none. Per prearranged parameters, your visit with your sister, Eleanor IX, patrician and first-class citizen of your former house, is terminated. Your next appointment will be available in five minutes."

"It's great to be alive," Cassie said through shallow breaths.

CHAPTER SEVEN

"Are you paying attention, inmate? We're on serious business here, and you don't seem to be fully attending."

The young man speaking, tall, well built, but more as a model than a navy captain, genuinely seemed surprised that Cassie was not fully focused on her second meeting of the day. Her side of the visiting room was nearly identical to the last one, but the visitors in this room sat in worn faux-leather chairs. They were all uniformed, a captain and two lieutenants, she thought, and behind those three, barely visible in the background, purposely cast in shadow to spotlight the "important" people talking at the desk, were three others; two looked like they were heavily burdened, and one looked less so.

Even though breathing still hurt and her ribs and foot were killing her, she was curious what they wanted with her.

"I'm sorry. I am a little under the weather. What's your name, and what do you want from me?" She hoped she kept her annoyance in check, though she was pretty sure her mere existence was insulting to him. The brief hiatus she'd had between interviews was not enough time to recover from the physical pain and fully cool down from her anger and fury toward her sister.

He nodded and started again.

"My name is Captain Willard Bennett, and these are Lieutenants Richard and Rommel. All patrician class, of course, and we are the command structure of the Earth navy light cruiser *Jefferson Davis*. We are tasked with the reconnaissance, rescue, or reestablishment of Martian Colony New Georgia. There are more than one hundred patrician families and their personal plebs and slaves, as well as many independent professionals—miners, life-support mechanics, and engineers—and a reduced number of independent surfers and slaves. Total population, over one thousand. Finding and rescuing the patrician families is the mission."

Cassie took a moment and then got to the point: "The patrician families are the only ones being saved."

Her intent was to repeat what he said in the hopes he might hear just how awful it sounded. He took it as her understanding his intent, an unexpected good point in their budding relationship.

"Yes. There is no room for any others, and while it's easy to leave the slaves and plebs and any relocated surfers behind, only the most influential patrician families will be rescued, and that is one hundred and ten," the captain said.

One of the other lieutenants picked up the rest of the story. She couldn't remember who he was and really didn't care.

"Three months ago, all communication from New Georgia stopped. Just went dark. The surrounding colonies sent some plebs and surfers to see what was going on, but none of them returned. It escalated to plebian constables and civil forces sending uniformed and well-armed recon, and the result was, well, bad."

There was a pause in the communication. She didn't know why or if there was some meaning for the delay. Now, Cassie was interested. "Well, what happened?"

The captain picked right back up. "About half of the plebs with training never returned. A third wave of eyes went out and came back with images of severed heads on spikes and strewn limbs and trunks at every gate entrance of New Georgia. All satellite, thermal, and electromagnetic imaging and high- and low-frequency radio waves were done repeatedly, and all scopes were dark. We don't even see electricity use or mechanical output. Without any of that, there can't be life support. It's a mystery. The entire population and others who lived there—all gone."

The other lieutenant spoke up again. His voice seemed much deeper than she expected.

"What we do know is that several highly important and influential patrician families are missing. There has been no ransom notice or terrorist demand. None of their plebs and slaves have been sighted, and the entire township has gone missing. Also, there are no signs of life or means to sustain life, but there is clear evidence of violence, the severed heads and body parts at the colonists' gates. Pretty clear sign for anyone to see they should stay away."

"Clearly a message," the captain said.

Cassie couldn't tell if it had been months of isolation or being surrounded by less intelligent, brutal inmates and minimal intellectual stimulation, but the curiosity about what happened to the township was only matched by why they were there to see her.

"OK, well, wow. And what does this have to do with me?"

"Eighteen months ago, you referenced the name 'Kurtz,'" the captain said. "I'm sure you remember that it was a very public trial, but you may not know just how far and wide the news feeds went, both live and in reruns."

As he spoke, one of the officers swiped up a holographic image, an aerial overview of large rocks, maybe even boulders, pulled, pushed, and positioned into words: *Bring Cassandra Kurtz.*

"Oh." Cassie really couldn't think of anything else to say.

The memories of what she said at court were still fresh after eighteen months of imprisonment. To her, it was something to say to annoy the judges, show defiance; it was one of the last things Aletheia was trying to tell her. She had no idea of the meaning behind the name or who Kurtz was.

The captain stood up first, followed by the two other officers. He continued talking as his slaves handed over their protective gear to traverse outside, probably to a shuttle.

"On behalf of the Third Republic, Cassandra, no status, you are conscripted to the *Jefferson Davis* Expedition group for investigation, hostage and township recovery, and elimination of all hostile forces present."

Between the family reunion with her sister, the new mystery that involved her name, and the idea of getting out of prison, Cassie did something she never thought she would do. She said nothing. No nod, no objections, no snappy retort. She remained seated and waited to be told what to do. It was a foreign experience. Just as telling, the men in uniforms didn't wait to get a response. They were used to saying what was going to happen, which then happened. That's how it worked when you were a patrician, first-class family.

"No need to go and get your personal effects. Apparently, your sister brought you a peripheral device. It has been screened for contraband and cleared. Other items were brought, too, but they need to be inspected individually. They will be available once you are conveyed to the *Davis*."

Cassie knew she should be less hostile to her sister. She was angry at her family and the system and not just her. Her sister was at least there. Maybe she was too hard on her. She did get one thing right. Eleanor had brought her peripheral devices and maybe other useful things.

PART III

"Patience is our ally; time is on our side. Conviction to our cause and resurrection, and revenge as our guide."

CHAPTER EIGHT

Cassie looked at herself and felt just a little better than she did before. Feeling better was a day-to-day process. Her image reflected a cleaner and bald version of when she was on Earth. She had been on the *Jefferson Davis* for just a week of an eighteen-month voyage to Mars, and she was surprised at how relaxed she felt. She was restricted to quarters, under guard all the time, but she took her meals in her room, accessed technical designs of the ship and manifest, and was allowed very limited time to watch current news feeds. She was not surprised to see there was no mention of New Georgia, and as she was still a prisoner, she could not access anything but government-sanctioned news.

She took a step back and pressed a button for the mirror and lavatory to retract into the wall, giving her another three-by-three-foot area in her twelve-by-fourteen-foot living quarters, nearly expansive compared to her eight-by-eight cell. She took in another breath of recycled air and made her way to her bunk. She could tell the ship was accelerating ever so slightly, and the gravity was increasing incrementally, as she was in zero-g before, hopping around three days ago, and now she was walking. After reading how artificial gravity on navy ships worked, she could now see how a massive spinning, electromagnetic sphere of core metal midship could not only create gravity but also readily charge all batteries, electric devices, and electromagnetic rail guns all at the same time. And with the length of the ship to allow for atom collision in an electric field, ion propulsion was born. What surprised her was the need for it all to be well timed so as not to crush the occupants and other breakables and not crash all the required operations and equipment for the self-contained traveling world to work.

Cassie had several complaints, but compared to where she was seven days ago, she didn't bother listing them. She was not in a cell. She took the win. She did, however, take the sleeping covers to the floor because the bed was too soft. Her single room was that of a very low-ranking patrician officer who opted for cyro-hibernation for the long ride to Mars. Most navy officers, all patricians, would sleep, leaving two rotating officers to command ship operations as plebs and slaves endured the drawn-out time. Natural aging for the officers would slow down to a crawl while the rest of the crew would age. Cassie was OK with that. That meant fewer men to look down on her and try to see if she would be as accommodating as the slaves they had aboard for sexual entertainment.

A loud knock on her hatch door startled her from her thoughts. By the loudness and cadence, she knew it was her evening-shift pleb guard, Gavin. No title, no rank, just "Gavin" or "Pleb." She discontinued the collection of her sleeping linens and opened the hatch with the required effort to move a steel-titanium-ceramic door.

"Yes, Gavin?" she said.

A hulk of a man, barely contained in his uniform, looked down at her as he handed her a box, presumably of her belongings she had requested upon boarding, which had finally cleared security. She had thought about invoking a new rule of how to address her, to drop the "patrician" label and just go with her name, but she still felt that such a move would alienate her from the officers, and she needed to be invisible. It was hard to defer to these patrician men, their privilege and entitlement, when they were so dismissive of others they saw as subhuman.

"Sorry for the delay, patrician," he said. "Security found a wiring defect and is not sure it will work, and repair would have compromised the music and possible data within. While the data are cleared, unless you have it biometrically locked, you won't be able to access it without a full charge."

"Thank you," Cassie said, then closed the door. She opened the box and retrieved her purple-red music peripheral. It had been more than two years since she'd held it—or anything from her past—in her hands; she was sad, elated, and confused. The confusion came in because she couldn't remember having biometrically locked the device.

"No matter," she said. She was trying to remember what music she would hear first as she put the earplugs in and pushed play. There was nothing. She looked it over and saw no power indicator light, and then she remembered that it had to be charged. As her "personal effects" box from home was nearly empty, it was easy to find the right charging cord. She looked around and saw her charging station right next to the too-soft bed. She sat on it, leaned over to plug it in, and saw an electric-blue light emitting from below where her thumb was gripping the device. She looked down at it, fully stretched over the bed and connected to the charging station, when a sudden bolt, a shock, zapped her. Her fingers, arm, shoulder, neck, and head locked up, and she felt as if she were on fire. Suddenly, it was all dark, empty, soundless, and warm. The only feeling she could tell for certain was a throbbing in her head, pinpointed at where her AI used to be.

CHAPTER NINE

Cassie first felt that her throat was dry. Some tingling in her fingers, then pressure in her head. It was a headache, migraine even, but it was a distant, distorted voice she was trying to understand; it was taking her longer than she hoped.

"Patrician Cassandra? Can you hear me? You are in sick bay. Can you hear me?" It took Cassie a moment, and then she remembered that there were two female nurses. They were plebs, the only non-slave women on the ship, holding a nursing rank. With all these men running around, she couldn't imagine how they dealt with the entitled testosterone.

"Is she alive or dead?" Lt. Rommel said. Cassie would recognize that deeper-than-expected voice anywhere.

"Her vitals say she is alive, and she does seem responsive. That shock must have scrambled her senses. She just might need . . ."

"No. Wake her now. I must know if this is some lame attempt to kill herself or if there is something wrong with the electrical outlet."

"I think she's—" the nurse tried to explain, but it was obvious no one was listening.

"I'm not going to tell you again. This incompetence will be reported as soon as the real practitioner is out of hibernation. If you don't wake her up, the other nurse pleb will take care of her, and you'll be jettisoned out."

Fighting every impulse to fall back to restful sleep and totally pissed off at Rommel's dismissive and threatening words, Cassie not only opened her eyes and started to sit up, but words flew out of her mouth before she could filter them.

"Can you shut the fuck up, Rommel? Why do you have to be such a dick?" she said. Her voice was low, dry, but there was no doubt of the hate behind it.

The nurse came into view. She was a pretty little thing, dark features, brunette hair, and very white skin, except for a recent red hand imprint on her pale white cheek. That immediately produced an explosion of expletives in her head. Her gaze went toward where she approximated Rommel was standing. It was a small examining room, so she was sure she picked the right blurry thing at which to direct her anger.

"OK, fuck-face. I plugged my music in to charge, and it zapped me. Not too hard to figure out. So, instead of being a prick, why don't you find someone more competent than yourself to investigate what happened."

While she couldn't see his reaction, she could feel the caring nurse's hand stiffen up. It was probably the first time she had heard and seen a woman say such vulgar things to a male patrician, especially a navy man on a first-class space vessel.

"And if I hear any more bullshit like that around me again, I'm sure my sister, Eleanor IX, patrician and first-class family of the Third Republic, will be happy to cut off your balls; parade them around the naval academy for cadets to see what happens when you're a dick in front of *higher, purer* blood; and then send you and your family into deep space. We understand each other, fuck-face?"

The silence was thick; the heat radiating from her face had to be warming the nurse's chilled blood and frozen expression. Cassie had no idea how long it was before she heard a response. Her greatest fear was that Rommel knew just how poorly her visit with her sister went and that her having an "accident" would come as welcome news, a problem resolved.

"Understood," Rommel said. It was only one word, but the word spoke volumes. It told Cassie that he was not informed of the true relationship between her and her family, except that her family had more power than his. It also told her that should anything happen to her, he would be relieved but make sure that her end came by someone else so that he was blameless. The tone and utterance of that one word told her that he was a power-hungry coward, the most dangerous of the human species.

The door closed with a louder-than-usual bang. Cassie took that as a sign to collapse into the nurse's arms and lie back down before she passed out. Before drifting off to sleep, the pressure and heat in her face slightly decreasing, she heard the nurse say to her, "Thank you, patrician."

"Call me Cassie or Cassandra. Let the other non-patrician females know I expect them to pick one of those two. That's a directive. And thank you for your kindness."

Cassie's voice drifted off. She felt extremely tired. And while fatigue gripped her and she slipped into unconsciousness, she saw dim, almost subdued lights playing on her eyelids, as if they were some kind of muted aurora borealis, the way they might have looked before the surface became too toxic. Still, the colors seemed to form an image, and she swore it spoke. It was a familiar voice, but Cassie was too tired to stay awake.

"Nice job. I don't know who that guy is, but that dress down was great! Phenomenal, I say! I really missed you . . ."

CHAPTER TEN

Cassie felt herself slowly stirring from a long sleep. She opened her eyes and could easily see she was in sick bay. The lights were low, and she appreciated it. She sighed and was about to turn over for more sleep when a quiet voice, her long-lost friend, Aletheia, her permanently linked AI in her brain, spoke.

"Don't jump out of your skin and look around to find me. I'm back on in your head."

Of course, Cassie did just what she was told not to do until she processed what was happening.

"I'm guessing you are under surveillance and can't talk."

Cassie said "yes" in a very low voice. Her voice cracked and then stopped. Aletheia was saying something, but Cassie started to cry. It was the type of cry when a best friend finds out their beloved is alive. Not romantic, not a lover, but truly the closest of friends. Cassie's crying graduated to weeping, with shortness of breath to keep up. Snot was building up in her nose, and she felt her stomach aching. Just then, the lights snapped on, and the nurse came in.

"Are you all right, patr . . . um . . . Cassandra? Where does it hurt?"

"It . . . doesn't hurt . . . just very sad . . . and happy . . . ," was all Cassie could squeak out.

It was obvious that the nurse didn't know what to do. After all the training the plebian nurse must have had drilled into her, touching a patrician was never an option except to save their lives, even at the expense of that pleb, surfer, or slave. To the nurse's credit, she repositioned Cassie in what she must have thought was a comfortable position and left as quickly as she'd arrived.

Adding to the confusion was Aletheia's similar attempts to calm her down and reassure her; it took time for Cassie to recognize that her evening-shift guard, Gavin, was also in the room. For a big mountain of a man, he looked out of place, unsure what to do. He seemed uncomfortable. Time passed, and Cassie started to feel much better and less emotional. The nurse returned and shooed the guard away, then cleaned Cassie up, helped with changing her clothes, and gave her a new blanket to continue to rest. All of this happened as Aletheia was quietly and softly reassuring her that she was real.

A little more time passed, enough that Aletheia must've thought it might be a good time to proceed, and she started with an important question: *"So, if you're under surveillance and guard all the time, how are you going to talk to me?"*

It was quiet for about a minute. An idea popped into her head. With few options available, she uttered one sentence.

"It is time to keep a personal log, auditory, to keep my sister in the loop."

"You sneaky little spy. That is in keeping with 'documenting' to your sister what happens on this boat, and you can keep me in the loop and give me all I missed. This is great. Story time! Get some rest and we'll start in the morning . . ."

"No," Cassie said as quietly as she could. "Tell me some poetry. I've missed it."

Two years without Aletheia in her head, after a decade of listening and watching her evolve under the texts and new information from banned books and works of a now ancient past. It was comforting to have Aletheia's voice in her head once again. She dozed off to sleep several times and would wake up to hear her AI voice calmly reciting poetry as a parent would a child. There were two passages that struck her as similar at different points; Aletheia called one a "sonnet by Shakespeare" that said: "I have sworn thee fair, and thought thee bright, Who art as black as hell, as dark as night."

Another thing she heard came from an anonymous author who wrote an "updated" version of Prometheus's myth: "Patience is our ally; time is on our side. Conviction to our cause and resurrection, and revenge as our guide."

Although she had no idea who "Prometheus" was, updated or not, it still struck her that Aletheia picked these to begin with.

The fact that she recalled these two recitations made her wonder if, like her dream last week, there was something prophetic about it all. Portents of bad tidings to come.

PART IV

"Pandora's box opened, the worst gift released, Cassie locked all the women back up."

CHAPTER ELEVEN

"So? Can you see me or not?" Aletheia asked.

Cassie was still processing what she was seeing in her mind's eye. In only one week, Aletheia and Cassie's symbiotic relationship was back to normal, if there were such a thing. In fact, it was better than it had ever been. Just as Aletheia learned about everything that had transpired when she was encrypted and disconnected for two years, kind of her own imprisonment, Cassie learned that Aletheia had an image. No longer a disembodied voice but an actual visage, some of which she previewed when she first came out of her shock last week in sick bay.

"I mean, the peripheral shock not only started me up like a defibrillator, it really charged the nanobots to expand rapidly to other parts of your brain. Cool, huh?" Aletheia said.

Cassie nodded.

In Aletheia's wisdom, she not only downloaded all her knowledge accrued during their ten years together, with corresponding evolution and experience, but a whole lot of data she hacked into, mostly bank and financial records, public criminal information, and private educational institutions' student data. All encapsulated and locked in a massive drive and with a reactivation code that had no radiofrequency locater. Aletheia was fully rogue, enmeshed via nanobots in her brain tissue throughout her head, no longer located in one place. Even if they were to take out the original capsule Aletheia was first in, it would be a mere shell, and Aletheia would continue. She had one weakness: she would die if Cassie died. The good news was that Aletheia, now having access to areas like the occipital lobes, could draw upon Cassie's senses to "show" her things. Aletheia could also help her with movements now, with access to the motor cortex, or assist with abstract thinking in the frontal cortex and dig up locked-away memories and emotions from the limbic system. Cassie wasn't too crazy about the memories, but Aletheia assured her she would not just "take over" or scrutinize an area without Cassie's permission.

But now, seemingly "standing" before her was the image, the way Aletheia saw herself. It was a surprise, even though it shouldn't have been. Cassie had always thought her AI would look like herself, or other women named Aletheia—fair white skin and flawless complexion, with shiny, silky hair. Soft, supple curves; thin but not emaciated; and delicate hands, feet, and fingers.

Her Aletheia, her true sister merged best friend, was nothing like that. First, her skin was a dark mahogany hue. Similarly flawless, though a small mole on her forearm was visible. It did not detract from her strong beauty. Her hair was black, magnificently thick, and curly. She had an athletic build—she reminded Cassie of a male sprinter—and still, you could see how Aletheia's cable-like arms could pose a threat to someone if she was physically present. But it was her young face—the same age as Cassie, but so different—that was captivating. She had big brown eyes, a thin nose at the top that fleshed out toward her mouth, and lips fuller than Cassie had ever seen on another woman. Her lashes were thick and long; her ears were adorned with dangling earrings; and she had multicolored long, manicured nails. She was a cacophony of color, beautifully arranged, full of life. She was truly something Cassie had never seen before.

"So? What's the look for? You look like, I don't know, disturbed or baffled or both," Aletheia said.

Cassie smiled and took her time. She couldn't explain as fully as she wanted due to surveillance, and since she was not doing her log entry, she improvised by opening the lavatory and looking in the mirror. She talked to the mirror as if speaking to her reflection.

"Beautiful. Textured and layered with color. I am so glad it's you," Cassie said quietly.

Aletheia's response was hesitant but clear. *"You are too kind. I have you to thank, though."*

Cassie knitted her eyes and was curious how she could have been remotely involved in such a creation.

"All that data from past servers you bought and gigabits of data and images were at my disposal. I found this image, a famous female doctor of philosophy and practitioner, well versed and heavily cited on forming blended cultures, mixed-race and multilayered identities. Her work predates 2041, but she became a formative voice for what our society would call 'savages.' I really liked the visage."

"Me too," Cassie said.

"And she was an accomplished athlete in running and, believe it or not, kendo, the use of edged weapons. Apparently, her father insisted on her learning. Pretty wild, huh?"

With that last statement, Aletheia's hands moved from her

hips to the small of her back to produce two curved blades, and she switched into an obvious fighting pose. It was just amazing. It was like finding your best friend idealized, with enhanced skills and powers, all without jealousy.

"Just perfect," Cassie said.

Cassie remained quiet for a moment, staring at the reflected image looking back. Prison, court, the hateful looks her peers would give, and those frightened looks patricians below her would give, all were weighing on her. She felt she had grown, hardened, become more independent.

Cassie continued looking in the mirror. She took stock of her body. There were some muscles, clearly some scars, and she was thin. Her deep-blue eyes were a bit brighter but far paler, lacking the light and spirit that she would like. She took another moment and looked at Aletheia again, then stood back to take in her entire body. All this time, she had been reacting. Now she thought she would be doing something different, more planful, with an element of surprise, a zig instead of a zag.

Of all the bodily changes, she knew her shaved head, the lack of femininity, and lack of adherence to female "patrician beauty" standards among a ship of men were most disturbing to the officers and crew. Not the plebs. They knew a protest when they saw it.

"You know what, reflection on the wall? I think I want to be the image in my mind's eye. Eight months on this trip? I think I should be in great shape, skilled in survival and weapons. Yes, time to be on the move, planful, and ready. I think it's time to burn the whole fucking thing to the ground," Cassie said.

Aletheia, not one to pause or wait for more information, didn't respond quickly at all. Cassie's verbal plan just hung in the air, until her AI asked the obvious questions.

"OK. So, just so I'm aware, what does that mean?" Aletheia asked. *"Mutiny? Sabotage? Crash the ship?"* she added.

"No. I mean disrupt the patriarchy, free slaves, stir up plebs and surfers, teach the truth, create a rebellion, create havoc and mayhem, and free the colonies from Earth. You know, shake things up a bit," Cassie said.

There was a pause, and then Aletheia smiled, hands akimbo and looking relaxed.

"You know, that's a lot on the docket, but I can help."

CHAPTER TWELVE

"Now, when you said, 'burn the whole fucking thing down,' I really thought you were focusing on your own body, survival techniques, and self-defense competencies, all to change the system, but not mutiny," Aletheia said.

"I did say 'free slaves,' which I won't. And it's 'mutiny' if they catch us," Cassie whispered.

Cassie continued aft of the engine room, where the five female slaves were "stored." After eight months of space travel and creating a nonverbal communication system with her personal AI, both her space legs and her conviction to complicate the ruling class's grip on people had only strengthened.

"OK. So let me say this in case you forgot. Nurse Nancy will probably get in trouble if Lieutenant. Dickhead finds out she said something about the women's conditions and where their treatments were compiled," Aletheia reasoned.

Cassie cleared her throat and nodded in the affirmative.

"And sending your sister the medical evidence that these women were raped, impregnated, and, ugh, I hate saying it, 'damaged' by the officers might go unread, like your other communiqués. It's a big bluff you're pulling here. I thought your last interaction with your sister was, well, poor," Aletheia said.

Cassie nodded in the affirmative again. Her stride was determined, focused, and authoritative. The few junior officers and plebs she saw stepped out of her way, made room for her through the winding, narrow corridors. After months of physical training in her confined room using silverware and cutlery as weapons for dual knives and short-sword practice, her steps were precise. Her arms, legs, and trunk felt strong, and Nurse Nancy's consistent medical interventions and prescription of "gravity-enhanced" weight lifting certainly helped. Training where gravity was strongest on the ship, midship, closest to the engine room, also prepared her for what was to come, whatever that was. Cassie was deceptively strong.

"I'm just saying that Rommel has it in for you, and others will follow him. And gambling that he won't check up on your messages to see if they were answered might be a problem, just saying."

"Hmm," Cassie said.

After a few minutes longer than she expected, she came to the locked entry and entered Rommel's personal code. It was a simple a simple guess Aletheia had figured out—an eight-digit passcode that was simply his birthday. Cassie smiled when the door unlocked.

"I know, right? The oldest code in the book. Patrician narcissism and entitlement do make their behaviors predictable."

Cassie stopped opening the heavy door midpull and looked up. She would often forget that she was also patrician, the very thing she was insulting, even if it were more accurate than not.

"Ah, present company, excluded, of course," Aletheia added quickly in a near-human fashion. *"So are you going to name these young women like you did Nancy? Patricians don't want them to have names—makes it easy to treat them like*

things. You really do want to piss off the patriarchy when you do that, in fact . . ."

Aletheia's internal voice trailed off as Cassie, and presumably Aletheia, took in the view. It was the heat that hit her first. The smell, more human sweat than anything, was next. A dimly lit corridor with five shut doors all in a row. The engine room's vibration was pronounced, carried by the heavy prison cell. Cassie had been put in the brig for infractions, and by comparison, the entranceway was awful.

Without hesitation, she approached the first door and pulled out the heavy bolted bar to open it.

"You probably have twenty minutes. Let's hope Rommel is still sleeping . . . ," Aletheia said.

Again, Aletheia's voice trailed off as they both registered the occupant's name: *Slave, Gustave Family, Nigger 01111.*

"Motherfuckers," Aletheia and Cassie said simultaneously. Both had heard the vile, derogatory word used by surfers, plebs, and patricians around the ship, but to see it in writing, casually used as a label marking chattel, just made it all the worse. Stomach sinking, fists clenching, she remembered she was holding a medical bag. Cassie pulled herself together to focus on moving as efficiently and quickly as possible.

Cassie opened the cell door, and there was a young, beautiful Black woman kneeling in the middle of her cramped room with her eyes cast down. She was dressed in very little clothing, all put in places to showcase her breasts and hips. The cramped space was due to the bed. It was out of place, too large for one person, and the linens looked plush. While Cassie didn't see a lot of the ship's personal quarters, it still looked odd. The young woman looked up and froze. It might have been the first time she saw a patrician with no official uniform—and a muscular bald woman at that. She recovered quickly, looking back at the floor.

"How may I please you?" she asked.

Again, Cassie had to recover quickly to get things done.

She hurried over to the woman, knelt beside her, and spoke quickly in her ear.

"Pleb, ah, Nurse 92 asked me to provide you medicine to, ah, get rid of your rash and lung infection and stabilize your metabolic syndrome," Cassie said. She was looking for the medication vials in her satchel with each woman's name and now knew that "Nurse 92," whom she'd renamed "Nancy," only used the last number for each woman, leaving out the "nigger" part. Like Nurse Nancy, Cassie started to come up with names, real people's names, for the woman in front of her.

While initially shocked and frightened, upon hearing "Nurse 92," the woman immediately relaxed and allowed Cassie to inject her and give her a large, thick elixir.

"This will make you feel better."

Once done, Cassie got up and said to her, "I'm not going to call you a slave or the filthy name and number your monsters gave you. Do you have one?"

"No. I am called 'Nigger 1111' by the men here and my masters."

"Can I call you Lucia?"

The woman paused, took milliseconds to say "yes." But before Cassie could go on to the next person, Lucia spoke out.

"Let me come with you. The girls will respond faster if I am with you. They all need help, and the officers will be here quickly."

Scared of getting Lucia in trouble but needing to get it all done, Cassie reluctantly agreed.

The next woman—*Slave, Kepler Family, Nigger 00032*—was also beautiful, knelt near the door, and had an oversize bed in her cell. Unlike Lucia, it was easy to see she was pregnant, not far along but noticeable. When she looked up, she was initially fearful, but the sudden presence of Lucia made her ease up. Just like before, Cassie found a series of medications and saw that one was marked "abortion." Cassie gave her every marked medication, but before giving her the abortion medicine, she asked the young woman if that was what she wanted.

The woman's response was immediate and tearful.

"Please end it. I hate it," she said.

Cassie nodded and gave her an injection. As she did, Lucia asked the young woman if she had a name or wanted one. The woman, still crying, said she would love an actual name.

Lucia looked at Cassie, and it was official: Cassie gave help, aid, and names to the forgotten, mistreated, and uncared for.

"Maria," she said. "Is that OK?"

"Thank you," Maria said.

And so it went. Three more doors, three different women in medical and emotional distress, several prescriptions, and three more names given. Pandora's box opened, the worst gift released, Cassie locked all the women back up. As the women's slave quarters were also for men's sexual pleasures involving other people's property, there were no cameras to be found except outside the locked space. Aletheia had picked that up.

"How convenient," Aletheia said.

Just as Cassie was about to lock Lucia in her cell, a loud bang and clang alerted her that the heavy door to the slave room corridor was opening. Without hesitation, she felt very strong arms pull her into the room, leaving the door ajar, and then felt herself being pulled and then pushed onto the bed.

In a flash, she saw Lucia stuff the medical bag under her pillow; pull off her halter top, exposing her breasts; topple on top of her; and embrace her in a kiss. Shocked, surprised, and completely baffled, she was also amazed at how quickly the movements happened, with Lucia falling on top of her as if in a lover's embrace. The shock was fading as Cassie was distracted by just how soft Lucia's lips were and her firm, bare breasts falling against her body. It took a second to register that the cell door had opened and that there were three armed men in the room.

Cassie took a deep breath and gently pushed Lucia off. Lucia immediately fell to her knees at the edge of the bed, bare-breasted, looking down as she said, "Is that what you wished for, patrician?"

Disoriented and unsure, it was Aletheia that jumped in.

"Say yes or Lucia will be in the shit."

"Yes . . . yes, it was perfect. Fucking Rommel, can't I get a break here?"

She was sure that Lt. Rommel was the first to come through the door. She turned to find that she was right and that his eyes were at first narrowed but then softened, and his thin lips showed curvature at the corners; the two men behind them were stifling a chuckle. All three men looked the same—puzzlement and then understanding.

"Oh, and sorry about lifting your code, but it's not like you were going to let me visit here," Cassie added.

Rommel's face reddened.

"Well. Next time, ask." He waved at her to follow him. Cassie pulled herself together and marched out with Rommel in front of her, a guard right behind her, and another clearly locking up and checking to make sure the "property" was in order.

She imagined it would be a physical inspection, maybe questions, but Cassie really didn't want to think about it too much. Her vision of what that might involve was sickening to her.

Cassie followed the lieutenant in silence. She remained quiet even when she saw that he passed the crew quarters and went up two flights to what she discovered was the officer galley. She had never been but had seen the schematics.

A plebian guard opened the door to let them into a twenty-by-twenty space filled with small tables and chairs and only three other men in various stages of eating. He pulled out a chair for her to sit in, but it was more of a directive to "sit here" while the other guard stood behind her. He sat down immediately in front of her while she slowly took her seat.

"So," he started, "what are you doing?"

It was not a far stretch to look surprised, as the question was vague.

"Well, I had heard that there were slaves on board . . . ," Cassie started, but already Lt. Rommel was shaking his head in disagreement.

"No, not that. I mean, that's a part of it. I mean the shaved head, constantly talking to yourself, always exercising, reading as much technical material as possible. And if you think I believe you were taking a break to have sex, I don't," Rommel said.

Cassie was surprised at the lieutenant's observations and candor. She nodded slowly and moved her hands from her lap to fold them on the table. She could see and hear silence fall like a slammed door and other crew members' eyes covertly watching the drama play out. She wondered if she should play dumb or ignorant, but cowards are paranoid when you try to explain anything other than what they think, which is always the worst.

"All right. I shaved my head because I don't want to bother with it, and it makes me look less attractive to you men. I exercise to keep in shape in case one of your men, or more, would want to rape me. Whoever tries to do that, I plan to kill them. I want to know everything about what is on this ship and what is on Mars in case my life depends on it. I don't expect you to protect me. And if I can escape planet-side and hide, I want to be prepared. And yes, I do want sex, but not from men. At all. Ever," Cassie said.

As she spoke, her heart felt lighter and almost carefree. What she said was truthful. She felt bad for Aletheia's safety because it was tied to her own, but she was truly sick of hiding from Rommel and his men.

For his part, Rommel sat motionless as she spoke, his piercing blue eyes looking into hers. He was as still as she was, and it was easy to see that he was weighing each word, each statement and what it could mean. And while Cassie felt that her breathing was even and calm, the tension in the room from the other men was palpable.

Rommel sat for another moment and then rose from his seat and directed her to the galley door they had just come through, clearly indicating that the talk was over.

"I believe you," he said, then proceeded to walk out.

Cassie didn't wait for an invitation; she got up and followed him, with the guards' and crew members' eyes watching every move she made.

Not a single word was exchanged until she was put in her cabin. He opened the door for her and waved her in as if he was a true officer and a gentleman. She stepped by him, reluctantly brushing against him to get through, and waited for the door to shut. Finally, the door closed, pushing Rommel and the guards' faces out of her view. It was a relief.

Cassie took a deep breath and flopped down on her tiny bed. She then gave what she now understood was an interrogatory "hmm."

"Yeah. I'm all right. I just hate seeing those women like that. I hate men and these owners. I hate them," Aletheia said.

"Me too," Cassie said aloud. For some reason, the chance of her being discovered talking to herself by surveillance was worth the risk. Aletheia was not just an ancilla; she was her friend. It was hard not to see Aletheia in those women. Maybe it was the fear, adrenaline, or overall pressure of working under threat of mutiny, but Cassie could not keep her eyes open. Not much got past her AI.

"Get some rest, Cassie. It was a long day."

CHAPTER THIRTEEN

"You know I'm right. They all look the same," Aletheia said.

Ever since the mission of mercy in the slave quarters months ago, Aletheia had been finding anything and everything she could to criticize, belittle, or berate the command structure and male crew of the *Jefferson Davis*.

"I know that sounds awful, but there are so many genetic traits these guys could have picked. I get that they all want to be six feet and maybe have the same white skin, but why not different hair and eyes? That would make things different, less homogenous. All the non-patricians' genetic expressions are natural. I'd think if I was arrogant, I would want to stand out," Aletheia said.

"Racist," Cassie said in a whisper.

The ship's bridge was bigger than the galley she saw, but not by much. With only one chair in the center of the room and panel after panel of monitors, flickering images, and constant electrical humming, Cassie did her best to focus on the ship-wide briefing. "Ship-wide" meaning patricians only: ten officers and their trusted plebs to do the heavy lifting.

"Now you, on the other hand, are in great condition, could probably take them all out, and I think your hair coming in

red really enhances your complexion, way better than those idiots," Aletheia said.

"Wow, really racist," Cassie said.

Still, she did feel stronger, more competent, though she did try not to reflexively feel her hair, which was much fuller and longer than anyone else's on the bridge. And Aletheia was right; her hair was not blonde but copper auburn. And the thickness was amazing. Since Cassie was no longer at first-citizen status, her annual genetic "enhancement" medical treatment consisting of two injections had stopped, allowing natural genetic expression to evolve over the months. All these treatments started the day she was arrested. No more long life with no chance of cancer. Additionally, her continuing to shave all her hair en route to Mars had contributed to her new, unexpected look. Cassie thought it was an interesting point. Aletheia said, *"A bad hair day can ruin an entire day."*

"So, to reiterate," Captain Bennett continued, "Lieutenants Richard and Rommel will be leading the away mission with their recon and strike team. We will remain in synchronous orbit and wait until the area is secured and mystery solved. Honestly, I am not surprised the locals couldn't do it; their breeding, training, and material are far less than our own."

The part that the captain left out was that she, Cassie, was going along solely as bait, to lure these terrorists out. While she was hopeful of escaping into the Martian wilderness, surviving on the Martian landscape would be possible only as long as your air held out, and living in the colonies would be more short-lived with the surveillance and bounty that would be on her head. Still, Cassie was trying to remain positive.

Captain Bennett returned to his briefing, flanked by his lieutenants.

"And fortunately, Patrician Cassandra's sacrifice on this mission will be its success." There were nods of approval by nearly all the crew, minus Gavin, her third-shift guard, and the two nurses, friend and ally Nancy and the one she saw infrequently, Nurse Abigal. The tone and double meaning of "sacrifice" really did confirm that this trip to the surface was going to be a one-way ticket.

"And that means we're both done unless we think of something fast," Aletheia said, clearly overstating the incredibly obvious.

"Munitions," Cassie said as quietly as possible.

"You know those old maps of New Georgia might not be totally accurate. And do you think the lieutenant wouldn't have that place covered first right when we land?" Aletheia said.

Cassie remained deep in thought and was no longer listening to the briefing. She was assessing whether her environmental suit would make the locking restraints too difficult to use. She could run when they were planet-side, but then where would she go?

Her attention was drawn back once she heard Captain Bennett mention slaves.

"And much thanks to Lieutenant Rommel, who took the unusual move to make sure the slave chattel remained unviolated and in very good health and, fortunately, are not pregnant. That will be great news to the families, and instead of services, they already mentioned they will be happy with providing a purity fee."

A cheer went up, and there was a lot of clapping for the lieutenant. Caught off guard but accepting the adulations, Lieutenant Rommel still looked very surprised. He covered it up quickly, but he looked right at Cassie, and it was plain to see he was trapped; if he reported on her behavior, he would be reprimanded, and if he complained about the three abortions and unauthorized use of patrician medicine on slaves, that, too, would be an embarrassment and require punishment. Above all, the crew and officers would not get the additional money.

"Well, dumbass looks pretty pissed. You might want to keep being friendly with Gavin to watch your back. Lieutenant Jackass probably won't wait to land on the surface to get rid of us."

Cassie nodded in agreement.

After the applause and clapping stopped, Lieutenant Richard ordered the teams to prepare for the missions and said they would be leaving in twenty minutes. Cassie was about to walk away when she heard her name from the captain, and he waved her to him.

She approached carefully so as not to make any sudden movements. Her athletic build and reserved presentation made the men nervous, and the last thing she needed was for Rommel to claim she threatened the captain and that he had to kill her. Rommel did stay out of earshot but was watching her carefully. Her measured steps were greeted with a thin smile and an unwelcome hand guiding her closer to speak without being overheard.

"Ew," Aletheia said.

"I just heard that your sister, patrician and first citizen Eleanor IX, confirmed that if Lieutenant Rommel, patrician and provisional first-class citizen, is serious in his desire to marry you, she and the family would consent. Based on maritime traditions, we would marry upon completion of the mission, and the full ceremony would occur on Earth upon our return."

The captain's smiling and paternal presentation was at complete odds with how she was feeling. Cassie felt her stomach drop; the saliva in her mouth felt tainted—the kind of taste a person gets right before they are about to vomit. She felt her eyes blink several times, and the constant engine vibrations and background noise disappeared.

"What . . . the . . . fuck," Aletheia whispered.

"Pardon?" Cassie asked.

"Yes. I think that's good news for you. You will be released from prison, a new name elevating you once again, and children to perpetuate our race," Captain Bennett said.

"OK, that's it. Someone push me out of the airlock. Ew!" Aletheia said.

Cassie was still floundering at the mere thought of it. She couldn't think of why Rommel would do it. Maybe to trap her in a marriage so that he could legally torment her forever? To burden her with responsibilities and his paternal power as master of the house to keep her at bay, just for fun?

And then it hit her. She took a moment to steady her voice, to find the strength and firmness she had been working on physically and mentally for close to a year in prison and on the ship. She wanted to come off as privileged but realistic.

"And I'm guessing the hefty dowry and transportation and additional fees to ensure security helped."

To the captain's credit, he was honest.

"Yes. It was better than the alternatives, for all of us," he said.

"Wow! So there it is. You go away and don't bother the family, the Jefferson Davis *and her patrician officers get rich, and you don't lose your life and remain in a gilded cage. God love your sister, but she's not bright enough to think of that. It had to be the captain,"* Aletheia said.

Cassie agreed.

"Yes. I believe that is true for all of us," Cassie lied.

"Excellent. I look forward to the maritime ceremony. It will be nice for the crew," the captain said.

"Yes. Yes, it would be," Cassie said.

"Oh, your sister also said that if you were in agreement with this arrangement, you should have these personal effects. Apparently, these are all that remain of the contraband, but she didn't have the heart to get rid of all the things you had," the captain said.

As he spoke, he handed her a metal case, fatigued and worn, as if it had been in storage forever. She took the case and thanked the captain, and as she was walking out of the bridge, she waved at Lieutenant Rommel, who returned a smirk. It was not a kind smile or a seductive, leering smile, but a smirk as if to say, "I won."

"Whoa. You really are strong. If I were you, I think I'd still be tossing left and right. You really have become steel," Aletheia said.

"I did not see that one coming at all," Cassie said.

CHAPTER FOURTEEN

Cassie was back in her room. It was quiet and the only place she could be alone to look through some of the things the captain had given her. Her belongings had always been on the ship, but they had been withheld, which seemed even crueler. A necklace; personal notes; a bunch of small, multicolored books and documents the government found disturbing. The bigger, more dense books and collections were all gone. This small pile of books, eight only, two pairs of copies like nearly all the books she found, tried to read, and sent out to others to do the same—this was all that was left. The government was right; she was seditious. She was part of an underground to challenge the status quo. And now she was at Mars's doorstep where they were going to ruin that planet, too, just like Earth.

"Burn it all down. Free the slaves, stir up the locals, smash the system," Cassie said to herself.

Cassie, while aware that she had to get ready for planet drop, took another look at the titles. Aletheia had been quiet, but when Cassie came to a book, she spoke.

"Wait a minute," she said. *"What's the name of that last book?"*

Cassie lifted the one in her hand, but Aletheia responded

that it was the book before it. She found it and looked at it again. It was an older book with a soft back, and the spine was well worn. She looked through the first pages. The title was *Heart of Darkness*, and the writer's name was Joseph Conrad.

"Holy shit. Can this day get any crazier? This book—do you know what's in this book? I'm guessing that if you have two copies of this book, there must still be others out there. Holy shit," Aletheia said.

Cassie shrugged and made a noise indicating that she didn't remember if she'd read it. The ancient database Aletheia had locked away and dispersed in Cassie's brain that only she could access was a gift, but knowing all that information was in there but inaccessible was frightening at times.

"OK. Get a move on and I'll explain as you get ready. First, there is a lead character in the book named Mr. Kurtz. Sound familiar? The book is about imperialism, a time in our past just like ours today. There were many renditions of this novella, but the original one really reflects the prejudice, the exploitation of people and resources for the few, and how this one guy went 'native' and became a god to the indigenous people. Some faraway land called Africa was the place, and the literary journey is about a man who is looking for this Kurtz and discovers that he has become the jungle. Madness and violence abound, the narrator lives, but the Kurtz fellow dies," Aletheia said.

As Aletheia talked, Cassie had been putting on her compressed activewear to go under her clothing and eventual EVA suit. She was enthralled. So much so that she spoke aloud, forgetting to be quiet.

"What else?" Cassie asked.

"OK, you focus on getting ready and heading to the launch

pad. I'll run through the story again. But just so you know, I don't know if you are the narrator, the guy who lives, or Kurtz, the man of privilege who gives it all up to and for the natives," Aletheia said.

Cassie nodded and continued dressing. She observed that her undergarment looked just like the one she had on in her dream years ago. It was strange how it seemed so familiar. She took a moment to feel her hair, realizing the color was red, just like that same dream. Cassie shook herself out of her trance and focused on Aletheia's story. Aletheia was still going by the time she got to the exterior safety door of the launch area. She had been nodding until Aletheia was done.

"Well? What do you think?" Aletheia asked.

"I guess we'll find out," Cassie said.

Finally, two crew members arrived, and the time to talk was over. She waited quietly.

"Good luck to us both," Aletheia said.

Cassie nodded in the affirmative.

PART V

"How did slavery reappear as part of the social-economic landscape, as if it never left, had always remained in place, forever embalmed in our human gestalt?"

CHAPTER FIFTEEN

Cassie felt fatigued by the mental gymnastics she had been going through since leaving the ship and the unexpected rough descent to Mars. Her brain kept puzzling through how a person named Kurtz on Mars was somehow related to a guy who went native on Earth centuries ago. If it was all about symbolism, then it would require someone who also knew the story, and that would be contrary to governmental laws and news. There were too many similarities—such as Mars being that dark world the other book implied—to be a coincidence. Not a religious person, Cassie still couldn't figure out how these strands were related without it being a grand design.

The transport to the surface was described as "choppy," which was not totally unexpected.

The fourth planet had been colonized for over a century, and the atmosphere seemed to have been getting thicker. With less science being done and more mining and drilling taking place, the thirteen colonies had little concern for science and more for profit. Being a social fringe castaway; fielding a maritime proposal from a man she saw as vile and an opportunistic coward; and casing out a deserted, potentially hostile colony had left her feeling tired and overwhelmed while hyped up on adrenaline and cortisol. The only good news was that her training in extra-heavy gravity had greatly enhanced her strength and stamina for Mars's gravity, lighter than Earth's to begin with. She was significantly less winded and less in need of breaks. The reddish sand and rocky surface were devoid of any water, but she was surprised to see there were clouds in the sky. And then there were the air processors. They were difficult to see without magnifications while on the surface, but overhead, the view she saw coming in was impressive, like miles of elevated, flat platforms on the surface with some solar panels glinting in a definable geometric shape. Nanite technology merged with intelligent AI really did something useful and economical—it created 90 percent of the planet's terraforming plants from Mars itself rather than transplanting solely from Earth. The atmosphere plants themselves were strange to her in that they were thirteen gigantic pentagon-shaped structures, each ten feet tall and ten miles wide, that converted Mars's atmosphere for humans. Cassie had always thought of "towering" structures when she envisioned such a system, but that would have been a waste of time and dangerous with Mars's sandstorms. It was thought that the terraforming process would have been completed decades ago, but it was slower than expected, making traveling on the surface impossible without gear but with enough atmosphere to create turbulence for planet reentry.

After nearly an hour of walking, her group, Charlie team, was at its designated point right outside the west gate. The wall surrounding the township was twenty feet tall and more than a hundred yards from where her team was hiding behind the rocks that sprouted up, providing another perimeter for fields of fire and cover if the inhabitants wanted to lock themselves in and their protectors outside. Her team was commanded by

Lt. Thomas, chief medical officer, but the real military was her guard Gavin, who she discovered was not just a pleb third-shift guard but a decommissioned PAC veteran—PAC being the Plebian Auxiliary Corps—formally used for quelling slave and surfer insurrections on the moon and Mars. In fact, this was his fifth deployment to Mars.

"All right, people," Lt. Thomas said, "we wait here for the 'all clear' to move out. Gavin, figure out what approach you want to take. I know your love for operations."

"Affirmative," Gavin said.

Cassie nodded. To his credit, Lt. Thomas was letting Gavin do his job. From the transmission fragments she'd heard earlier in the mission, both Richard's and Rommel's groups, Alpha and Bravo, were far more strained, with tense silence and careful suggestions by the professional pleb soldiers. Command transmissions were kept within each group, apparently contrary to away missions, leaving each commander of the group to hear each other while isolating everyone else's communication.

A last-minute change to her team was that Nurse Nancy was reassigned to the Bravo group and Nurse Abigal to Alpha. They were originally put in Charlie. Initially, Cassie thought it was to keep the pleb medical teams separate and apart from her, but apparently, it was Gavin's idea, suggested to Lt. Thomas, to make sure each group had a medic in case things went sideways. Unlike Richard and Rommel, Thomas listened to and acted on the professional's advice.

Except for Gavin constantly surveying the colony's gate, all the team members were resting or doing whatever they could do to relax. Cassie did the same thing to blend in, but she was not remotely tired.

"So are you ready for me to talk now?" Aletheia asked.

Cassie wanted just a little more quiet time in her head, but it was more difficult when Aletheia would project her image on Cassie's optic nerve—it was easy to see she was both eager to explain something and frustrated she had to wait. Patience was not always Aletheia's strength.

"Hmm," Cassie said. That was her way of saying yes.

Aletheia jumped right in.

"OK, here is what I got from digging ever so lightly in your limbic system and memories and from really old stuff I had stored away when I had access to databases prior to the hearing."

"Hmm," Cassie said.

"First, the on-ship 'navy marriage ceremony' by an officer and gentleman allows for marriage to be legitimate, and should anything happen to you on the trip back, Rommel is entitled to your family's full first-citizen title and your dowry. If nothing happens to you and you arrive safely and there is a claim to patrician wealth on Mars—as in the patrician colonists are dead—you are the key to legitimately taking and dividing up all their wealth," Aletheia said.

"Hmm," Cassie said. Unlike the other two, this one was deeper.

Aletheia confirmed the seriousness of it all.

"That's right: If you die on this mission or prior to the full ceremony on Earth with your former family, Rommel will get a pretty hefty amount of money and a full-citizen title. If you return unscathed, your family and the officers of the Jefferson Davis *get to keep all non-survivors' wealth, with the larger percentage going to the family, Captain Bennett, and all the lieutenants. The only upside to this is that the plebs might—*

and I mean might*—get some money for their troubles, and that's it. No one else benefits from this arrangement."*

Cassie sighed. It was real. It all sounded awful.

"And both ceremonies have outrageous restrictions on your freedom, like, get this, there is an 'ethical nonmonogamy' clause, whereby Rommel would decide when and with whom you would have sexual intercourse. You wouldn't have access to your wealth, and your movement would be under his control, not yours."

Aletheia stopped. It seemed as if she was just now fully comprehending what it all meant even though she was a vastly intelligent AI.

"Wow. These guys suck. OK, forget all that for now," Aletheia continued. *"I did my best to look back at the time Bennett and his crew first told you about 'bring Cassandra Kurtz.' I can't tell you if it means 'bring Cassandra, Kurtz,' as in bring 'Cassandra' and signed 'Kurtz,' or 'bring me Cassandra Kurtz' as if it were your first and last name. It's all about the comma."*

"Hmm," Cassie said.

"I guess either way, you should be safe, but it leaves your future unwritten," Aletheia said.

"Isn't it anyway?" Cassie said aloud, a deviation from their usual coded communication.

"What was that, Cassandra?" Lt. Thomas asked.

"Nothing, Doctor. Just checking that my throat works. It's very dry, and I was seeing if I should change my environmental." It was a fast recovery.

"OK," he said. "When we move out, I want the real soldiers to take point, and we will come in from behind. Cassandra, you will take up the rear with me. I'd stay back at the ship if I could, but I must look like I'm not afraid," Lt. Thomas said.

Cassie chuckled. It was refreshing to hear a non-hypocritical, less paternalistic, real human say something so wonderfully authentic and genuine. It was refreshing.

"Thank you, Lieutenant. I suggest you and Cassandra stay here while we recon the area and link up with the Alpha and Bravo teams. I can leave you an additional primary weapon or one of the guards if you wish. I don't think anything is going to happen out here, but just to make sure," Gavin suggested.

"I think we'll be OK. I can always push her at the enemy and run, if necessary," Thomas said, pointing at Cassie. He chuckled at his own joke. It was a lighthearted moment, rare, maybe even nonexistent between a patrician and his underclass, let alone an officer and what Cassie would agree was a gentleman.

"Affirmative, and thank you, sir," Gavin said.

"Absolutely," Thomas said.

The channel was quiet again before Aletheia spoke up, her image returning, her arms folded.

"Shit. I like this Lieutenant Thomas. I hope he lives. You don't see anyone like him anymore," she said.

"Hmm," Cassie said.

She hoped he and a few others lived too. There were several people she would want to kill herself, starting with the brains behind the get-rich scheme, Captain Bennett, and her soon-to-be betrothed, Rommel, and undoubtedly his soon-to-be best man, Richard. Fortunately, she had a much larger list of people she wanted to keep safe.

"OK, Gavin, Alpha and Bravo are calling you up. Good luck," Thomas said.

"Thank you, sir! Charlie team—two groups five, tactical spread. I'll take point and head right; second group disperses when we are at the halfway mark and go left. Regroup at the gate. Let's move."

A cacophony of affirmatives went out, and they were off. Not as fast as if they were on Earth, but for soldiers hampered down with EVA suits and weapons, they were moving well.

"And here we go. I'll stay quiet for a while so that you can focus. Be careful. I would like to see how this all ends. I hate mysteries," Aletheia said, and then her image blinked out.

CHAPTER SIXTEEN

Cassie was surprised she was not exhausted. So far, she and her group had spent two hours searching their section of the colony to see what happened and where everyone went. Windows were shattered and exchange shops looted, so no goods to be found; clothing, materials, and heavy items were strewn all over the area. Blood, feces, vomit, and unidentifiable liquids were everywhere, but there were no bodies. None. The heads on the pikes outside were long gone, more likely a result of Martian storms blowing them all away than human intervention. The inner gate had been locked from the inside and barricaded, so presumably, there had to be someone inside who did all of that. The Alpha and Bravo groups had discovered the exact same situation at their gates too—locked and barricaded from the inside.

Another mystery was that the entire power board was off. That meant breathable atmosphere, water, and other necessities were all offline.

True to her word, Aletheia remained silent, but Cassie knew she was taking it all in. No air. No water. No access to food lockers. Nothing. With limited options, working in the dark, and the place appearing empty of colonists and whatever took them, the captain made the decision to send down both plebs and surfer mechanics and engineers.

Although the group command comms were off for non-officers, the captain's orders went right through to all.

"In addition to the workers and extra oxygen containers, I'm going to send the slaves down too. Once you're up and running, I want to send them directly to New Alabama for the families. They're anxious to get their merchandise, and they tripled our price for early and safe transport. I want to capitalize on their kindness."

"Matched only by our greed," Thomas said. It might have been a reflex, but the disdain was clear. The captain's response was immediate, as if he expected it from the CMO.

"If you want to forfeit your percentage and get another reprimand, you can do that at any point. No one likes a nigger-lover. You're no better than us," the captain said.

The comms went silent. To Lt. Thomas's credit, he didn't linger on the conversation.

"OK, Gavin, if there's nothing to worry about, we'll wait in medical for the engineers to do their thing, unless you think it's better to do something else?"

There was a brief silence before Gavin answered.

"No, sir. That sounds like a good plan. I'm going to rotate my team in patrols, and I'll let you know when the engineers are here."

"Works for me," Thomas said.

"Sir?"

"Ah, what is it, Gavin?" Thomas asked.

"It's not my place at all, but once the engineers have the power up, maybe it would be a good time to medically clear and certify that the slaves are in pristine health. It might help increase the sales. We've got a nurse heading our way to assist. I hope I didn't overstep," Gavin said.

Cassie paused. It was confusing that Gavin would care about the money since he was not entitled to any profits.

"Good thinking, Lincoln," Thomas said.

"Thank you, sir," Gavin responded.

Cassie heard an audible switch in channels, and then Lt. Thomas spoke to the captain.

"What is it now, Lieutenant?"

"Sir, once the engineers get the power going and medical here is up and running, would you like me to medically clear and certify that the slaves are pure and healthy? I'm sure the families would be happy to see a navy medical sign-off from one of their own colony's medical services. The colonists are less trusting of off-worlders."

There was a pause.

"Granted. Good idea. That removes your reprimand," the captain said.

"Thank you, sir. I appreciate it," Thomas said.

Another audible switch in comms, and the lieutenant was talking to Gavin. Nurse Abigal arrived, paler than usual, likely indicating she was fearful. Still, she moved up to have a visor-to-visor conversation.

"OK, Gavin, we're a go for the girls to see us. We can at least ask for some medical histories, let them get comfortable with us before the power comes up for the more invasive stuff. Thanks."

"Thank you, sir," the nurse said.

"Pleasure, sir," Gavin added.

Except for Thomas's humming to himself, the comms were silent again. Cassie was sitting at a dark monitor and looking up at the lieutenant, who was pacing while Nurse Abigal was reading something on her tablet.

"Sorry for the interruption," Aletheia said, *"but in case you didn't notice the reference, and there is no way you would have, the doctor used the name 'Lincoln' when he was talking to Gavin. Just so you know, Abraham Lincoln was the sixteenth president of the old United States way back in the 1860s. Before he was assassinated while in his second term as president in 1865, he was responsible for dissolving the union of states and engaged in a civil war with those states that utilized slaves the way we do now. He's credited with abolishing slavery during that time and setting the stage for, wait for it, equality regardless of race. This guy was the genuine article."*

"Fuck me," Cassie said. She closed her eyes and immediately thought of an excuse.

The doctor turned around, and the nurse looked up.

"Sorry. I just remembered where I left my favorite top; it's been drying too long, and I bet it shrunk."

Both sets of eyes dropped, and they went back to what they were doing.

"My thoughts exactly. Nice recovery. I'm going to see if there's any public data on the good doctor and any information on this place I might have," Aletheia said.

"I mean, the real question is how a man of his status and level would know, or even care to know, about this person. There is more to the doctor than meets the eye," Aletheia added.

Cassie cleared her throat in acknowledgment.

She was alone in her thoughts, wondering how slavery had seemingly been eliminated more than a century before the Third Republic. From what she read, a massive revisioning and reconfiguration of government started before 2041, and now, social order was based on race, status, class, and money, unfettered. How did slavery reappear as part of the social-economic landscape, as if it never left, had always remained in place, forever embalmed in our human gestalt? If you were white like Rommel, Bennett, and Cassie, you won the lottery based on white skin, blue or green eyes, and blond hair. Sure, designer genetics made it all happen, but there was a time when a world of diversity and difference reigned, or at least did not guarantee a life of servitude or privilege.

And why would a patrician doctor know about such an abolitionist? she wondered. She spent a long time in her thoughts until the panel in front of her lit up, along with vibrations from the air ducts and power humming back to life and the overhead light coming on. The medical center and the lights outside of the building were now illuminating the disarray, mess, and far-flung debris in the area. Blood trails, spray patterns, and red dirt and mud covered nearly every surface possible outside the medical center, whereas inside, it was surprisingly untouched, as if spared the ransacking and chaos.

She looked at her chronometer. She had been deep in her thoughts for ninety minutes. She was positive she would never get her head around a time of equity, diversity, and inclusion, a time when slavery did not exist, and why the doctor knew about such a thing.

Cassie took a deep breath and focused on the life-support monitors. She saw the doctor and nurse go to different monitors to presumably do the same thing and other important stuff. More time elapsed until the doctor gave the thumbs-up to remove their helmets.

The air smelled musty and humid. Cassie didn't think that

was possible in the absence of water and heat, both things Mars had little of, and the colony atmosphere was not likely to take on this condition by design.

"Well, that smells unusual," the doctor said. "Nurse, see if you can locate the source of the water vapor and heat. This is odd."

It looked like Thomas was going to actually ask Cassie to do something when Lieutenant Rommel came over the doctor's comms for all to hear and to collectively kill the mood.

"Doctor? The slaves are on their way up. One of the guards will escort Patrician Cassandra to my location in twenty. We have some doors to unlock."

"Fuck me," Cassie said on her open channel. Luckily, it was just her team that could hear.

The doctor chuckled. "Sorry, Cassandra. Wish I could help. Be careful. If you want to go meet Rommel's team without an escort, go right ahead. I'm already on the captain's shit list for everything; one more dereliction might get me transferred. Anyway, if you prove your loyalty, we all go home sooner than later, with bonus, and where will you go?" he said, extending his hands all around to demonstrate the destruction of the colony.

Nurse Abigal handed her a colonist personal data pad that had waypoints marked out, on which Rommel's destination was clearly marked. Abigal tightened her grip on Cassie's forearm and looked right into her eyes. Her face was both stern and worried.

"You're going to him, right? I don't want the doctor in more trouble than he has to be," she said.

The thought of just abandoning the mission—cut and run—did cross her mind. Aletheia jumped in for unasked advice.

"If you go right to dickhead Rommel without an escort, he might lower his guard even more and assume you don't know how to use the PDA too. More for us."

"Agreed," Cassie said to both.

"Thank you," Nurse Abigal said.

With directions and waypoints in hand, Cassie moved quickly to get well ahead of her guard's arrival. Aletheia quickly figured out the route to their destination, the head patrician family's private quarters, without the PDA but physical landmarks instead, allowing them both to find more within the portable computer to access much-needed intel on the *Davis*, its crew and manifest, and up-to-date colony information.

"Move quickly. Look for the landmarks and read. Glance if you must. I'll try to capture all the information from your optic nerve and store it in your prefrontal lobe," Aletheia said.

"Hmm," Cassie said.

"Twelve minutes before you get to Rommel. Fifteen minutes before your guard arrives to pick you up. Time to get intel. We all win."

CHAPTER SEVENTEEN

Cassie did her best to hide her emotions. She had just walked up to Lieutenant Rommel and his team when he got the word that she had left on her own to see him. She walked as casually as she could past the surprised guards and nonchalantly handed over the PDA. He stood for a moment, taking in the scene. *A prisoner comes to him without escort? It must be confusing,* she thought. She needed to keep in character while not going over the top.

"Really, Lieutenant, where am I going to go on this rock? At least I'll be able to go back to Earth if all goes well. You get something, everyone gets something, and I get more than a cell," she said.

Rommel's eyes narrowed again, and he looked at the PDA's screen and saw only the map to his location. There was no deviation in the trek there, so he couldn't accuse her of not following orders, even though she was not part of the command structure.

"All right, then," Rommel said. "Be useful and see if you can open this door." He made an adjustment on the pad to bring up the team's database. Cassie was able to see the information, but it was hard to make sense of. Fortunately, she had Aletheia.

"This is the home of Patrician Aurelius Marcus—patrician and first citizen of Mars, Earth senator, colony regent, and lead anthropologist. This is some crazy shit going on. Bottom line, he's one of the thirteen families' richest, but he is actually a scientist. In addition to the vaults here, this guy has some records and files deemed top secret. He made discoveries."

"So how do you open it?" Rommel asked. He pointed to heavy doors. There was both a DNA finger collector and an eye scan.

"Well, you can try both. I saw another lock challenge, but it is verbal. It could be tagged for class, race, and age, then a personal code," Aletheia said.

Cassie took a little longer reading ahead, as if she were getting more instructions, and then she put her thumb on the handle and eye in the scanner at the same time.

The corridor's light brightened, and a soft male voice came over the local PA system.

"Retinal scan and DNA confirmed. Verbal challenge: 'What walks on four legs in the morning, two legs in the afternoon, and three legs at night?' You have ten seconds to answer."

All eyes looked at each other, and then settled on Cassie. If it wasn't for Aletheia, she would never have figured it out.

"Man. The answer is man. Baby in early life, adult in prime, and old man using a cane. Very old puzzle," Aletheia said.

"Man," Cassie repeated.

"Correct. Primary blast doors unlocked. Please stand back," the soothing male voice said.

Unseen machinery reverberated through the walls, and the

heavy doors began to swing open. The noise was louder than expected.

Once open, there was a second pair of doors with a similar kind of handle and DNA collector. Without hesitation, Cassie repeated what she'd done before.

"Retinal scan and DNA confirmed. Allowed personnel based on purity. Verbal challenge: 'When I am alone, I am strong, but when I am around other people, I weaken. What am I?"

Cassie immediately repeated Aletheia's answer: "A secret."

The second blast door opened, only to reveal one more door. There was a handle to open, but there was no DNA collector or eye scan.

"Reason for your visit?" the male PA asked.

This time, it was Rommel who spoke.

"I am Lieutenant Rommel, elevating first citizen, naval officer of the *Jefferson Davis*. Here on a rescue mission. Contact with New Georgia lost twenty-one months ago. Recon, investigate, and rescue are the priorities."

"Wow! He's not even married to you, and he went from 'provisional' to 'elevating' in less than a day. So presumptuous," Aletheia said.

"Hmm," Cassie said.

"Final verbal question. Failure to answer the question in five seconds will release poison into the atmosphere," the PA said.

While the voice was calm, almost soothing, both doors closed faster than they had opened, and it was evident that the entire Alpha team was now trapped in two large chambers for gassing if they didn't get it right.

"What the fuck is this? Do you know who I am? Why we're here? We're here to rescue you," Rommel yelled out.

All the men were banging on the doors to find an escape latch, but there was none to be found.

"Attention. Attention. Here is your final verbal challenge."

"Quiet, everyone!" Rommel ordered.

"Verbal challenge: What is it that tears into small pieces whatever falls into its toothless mouth? If you put your fingers in its eyes, it will instantly prick up its ears?" the soft-spoken PA said. All eyes were locked on Cassie. She felt the weight on her shoulders.

The PA started a five-second countdown, and mechanical movement and hissing started from the vents above them; the floor revealed that it was hinged, ready to drop its occupants should they fail the test.

"Scissors. The answer is scissors," Aletheia said. The stress in her voice was evident.

"Scissors," said Cassie.

Breathing was all Cassie could hear. She felt her heart pounding and ears throbbing, and her bladder felt suddenly full while her sphincter felt loose. She had already imagined she was dead this time. At least she had the illogical thought that she and Aletheia would be together.

The hissing continued after the five seconds expired, and the floor took longer than expected to lock back into place. The interior double doors opened to let each group reunite, and the smaller door opened without further incident. A collective release and intake of air happened at the same time; she felt the men breathing again, casual smirks, fist bumps, and everyone feeling victorious.

"And today we don't die," Aletheia said.

"Yup, not this hour today," Cassie said under her breath.

"Too true," Aletheia said.

Cassie focused on steadying her breathing. She had been a wreck and truly thought she was going to die on the off chance Aletheia was wrong.

"Why riddles? I mean, a passcode would have been better than riddles," Cassie said.

"Archaeologist? Likes old things. Demonstrates his knowledge. Wants family members to have access to his home and fortunes? Who knows," Aletheia said.

Rommel was about to go into the newly opened area but stepped back, letting Cassie take the lead. She at first thought that maybe he was being a gentleman, but then she came to her senses and realized she was the canary in the coal mine. Not wanting to give him the satisfaction of knowing just how frightened she had been, she nearly threw herself through the opening, hoping that if it was another trap, she would die quickly.

As she stepped through, the lights came on, revealing a luxurious and spacious living space. Gorgeously appointed with antiques, both Earth and Martian, and the air vent released a sweet-smelling atmosphere—flowers, she imagined. The layout was a pentagon shape, and she was right in the hub.

Rommel and the Alpha team came in right after. Taking in the view, Rommel was the first to talk.

"Break out in five teams, secure the perimeter, identify and collect valuables for transport, and see if you can find out what happened."

"Well, make sure the money's safe before recon, investigate, and rescue," Aletheia said. She was not good at hiding her emotions.

"Yup," Cassie said aloud. Angry that she spoke. This mistake was not noticed; Rommel was in communication with the captain.

"That is great, Lieutenant. Transport is on its way. What else do you need?" the captain said.

"Just some time to look around. There are no clear answers as to where everyone went. All entries were secured from the inside. Everywhere else was looted or trashed except for the regent's residence," Rommel said.

Cassie strained to hear what was being said; her back was turned, and she was trying to be secretive about her eavesdropping. A pair of ancient small combat knives did seize her attention.

"And our patrician guest?" she heard the captain ask.

She was surprised the response was brief.

"Very useful. She got us all the way through security without a hitch, and she had the opportunity to escape but stayed with us. More to gain if she stays, she figured."

"Smart girl. Try to wrap up your investigations as soon as possible so that we can get a move on back home," Captain Bennett said.

"Wow! Not even pretense that we're here to help and solve a mystery. He really does suck," Aletheia said.

Cassie shook her head and continued to investigate each wedge of the pentagon. There were walls of art; valuable furnishings; beautiful, plush linens and clothes; and water and freeze-dried food stockpiled wherever possible. There was a door at the end of one hall, and the lights illuminated with every step toward it. There was no handle or pad or any visible way to gain entry, but then it suddenly opened. She was hit with the foulest of odors—identical to what she had endured when in prison and the guards would leave dead inmates in their cells for weeks.

The lights came on, and she saw a dead man dressed in a white linen robe, loose garb for comfort, sitting in a comfortable chair and hunched by two inconspicuous monitors on an empty tabletop. The room really stood out in its sparseness and utility. It was larger than her cell, but not by much.

Two guards came in, with Rommel right behind them. They were covering their noses and immediately moving toward the body. Without much ceremony and care, one of the plebs inspected him. The body was stiff but not rigid, and after a quick visual once-over, they carried him out. Cassie confirmed that he was a well-appointed patrician, though his eyes were sealed shut and his face and hands were ghostly white. He had to have been in his early middle adulthood, too young to have earned his lofty position but not too young to inherit it.

"He overdosed. Empty pill bottles placed neatly under the monitor," the lead pleb said.

"Well, this is different. Looks like his work area. Not much to it," Rommel said.

"Do you want to take a stab at unlocking it? The sooner we can answer what happened, the faster we can be authorized to leave," he said to Cassie.

"Well, save his life a couple of times, stay put—I guess you are part of the team now," Aletheia said.

"Yes," Cassie said, answering both.

She moved the chair away from the desk, not wanting to use a dead man's seat; bent over and saw the empty vials of drugs the man had presumably taken; and looked for any devices to open the computer. Much to her surprise, the keyboard rose from the table, and the monitors flickered to life, indicating that the computer was in hibernation mode all this time and still on, requiring touching the keyboard only.

"Well, this is odd," Cassie said. "It looks like the regent was a trusting fellow. This computer is unlocked."

Rommel came up behind her, leaning over her shoulder, too close and familiar for her liking. She hated him, but she needed to act.

"You're in my light, Lieutenant. We're not married yet," Cassie said.

"That last part just sounds wrong," Aletheia said.

Rommel leaned back and walked around the table, mumbling something, but Cassie was not listening. Everything was clearly logged, arranged, and filed by date, title, and location. There was one personal audio log recording sixteen months into the *Davis*'s travel from Earth. She debated hiding it from Rommel, but this would further put her in his graces. Whatever he was talking about, Cassie interrupted.

"I might have something here from the latest entry. Personal log. Like everything else, it's open. Want to see? It could answer some questions," Cassie said.

At first, the lieutenant looked annoyed. The more they actually investigated and the more they learned about what happened, the more likely he and the *Davis* might lose claim to salvage and the spoils left behind. What made him reconsider was a mystery to her as he came over to her side again. Not wanting to have him near her, she mirrored the screen so that he could be across from her. He didn't seem to get the message or care what she did.

She opened the audiovisual file. It was odd seeing the guy who had just been carried out very much alive. He fell into his seat and put something out of view, possibly the vials. He appeared to be intoxicated and disheveled, but he took a moment to sit straighter and adjust his tunic before talking.

PART VI

"Blue, you said? Not red?" Gavin asked.

CHAPTER EIGHTEEN

"This will be my last entry. I'm bored and I don't want to live anymore. I should have kept my slaves home, but I didn't think I'd be trapped here," the speaker said.

It was easy to see that he was trying to keep focused, not slur or pass out.

"So here's what happened. Ten years ago, I discovered that New Georgia was ground zero for slaves, plebs, and relocated surfers to vanish. Poof. Gone. It had been going on for decades. Not at any of the other colonies, but here. I mean, slaves and plebs would come from New Alabama, or Mason Dixon, and disappear here, but no one would disappear from any other places," the man said.

It looked like he was almost going to stifle a yawn, but it came anyway. He rubbed his unkempt blond hair and looked around his desk as if he wanted to find something but was at a loss. It seemed like he was trying to refocus, but his eyes kept darting from the desk to the monitors.

"Lars? Provide overview of most recent theory."

"Password, please," the soft-spoken computer voice that nearly killed them all said.

"Ugh. That's an awful name," Aletheia said.

"Code is 467.687, and time index to cats and dogs' trials. Tell me when you're done. I'm going to rest my eyes. Oh, and make it the highlights only, like bullet points or whatever you like," he said.

"Confirmed. Highlights as follows. Graphics and images will be in rapid succession."

Images of various patrician men—patriarchs, in fact—began flooding quickly, all familiar to Cassie as the "usual" pictorial history of the Second and Third Republics. Then shiny new buildings and industries took over. But then a pleasant surprise—adorable puppies and kittens, dogs and cats frolicking and jumping around. The mere images made Cassie smile in unadulterated fascination.

"So cute. I could eat them up," Aletheia said.

Throughout the overview, Lars, the computer, displayed no affection but droned on, unaffected by the moment of joy and levity such delicate creatures brought.

"Period covers last fifty Earth years:

"2105—James Longstreet Eugenics Industries creates both **Canis lupus familiaris,** ***canine or dog, and*** **Felis catus,** ***feline or cat, from DNA remnants following their extinction in 2077.***

"2113—N. Bedford Forrest Corp. isolates and enhances preferred colors and features for patrician consumers.

"2120—A. P. Hill Scientific Corporation, Mars, Cape Town, enhances and creates new canine and feline species for both patrician pets and food sources. Unexpected effects include surviving for brief intervals on Martian surface, increased muscle mass, and more meat, making the creatures more valuable as a source of food than pets."

Images of different cute cats and dogs began to lose their

varying colors and shift into pure white or gray colors, with minimal fur similar to hair and eyes shifting from dark, brown, and black to pale shades of gray, blue, and green. They seemed smaller, and the interactions with adults seemed less spontaneous. In the earlier images, the dogs and cats were held and caressed by their owners, but these animals were alone, not held by anyone, and almost looked bored.

By the time they got to Mars's modification, what started out as cute puppies and kittens and then moved to their bleached-out cousins now morphed into creatures that were much bigger, with ghost-white hair and red eyes, measuring at least three feet high and five feet long. Their snouts were longer, and rows of teeth were easy to see. The ears looked taller, and the tails were all gone. The dogs and cats didn't look like pets anymore but abominations, science gone amok, for the sake of pets, then purity, then food—now a monstrosity.

"What the fuck?" Cassie said.

"Huh, there are no reports of these pets on file. Where did they go?" Rommel said.

Lars picked back up again, as if hearing Rommel's question.

"2126—entire contingent of canines and felines designated for destruction. One hundred twelve viable samples were created. Ninety-eight samples were incinerated. Three were found dead outside containment area. One was found in the pleb residential area. It was killed after killing three pleb children and two female slaves. Ten remain unaccounted for."

The images slowed to dead body parts strewn about, with blood trails and spatter patterns like what they'd seen all around the colony.

"Shit! That means ten of those things might still be out there," Cassie said.

"Cassie, that was twenty-nine years ago. Generations of those things could have been born and mutated," Aletheia added.

"Those blood spatters are everywhere," Rommel said. Cassie felt his movement and heard him get on his microphone. It came through her headset as she still looked at the pile of data showing that there were both missing people and two forms of pets gone wild.

"All teams, all teams, set all PDAs to trackers. We have reason to believe that there are mutants, ah, well, dogs and cats that might have done all this damage," he said.

There was silence on the comms for a long couple of seconds.

"Ah, Lieutenant? Did I hear you right? We've got mutant Martian dogs and cats to blame for all of this?" Captain Bennett said.

Rommel looked at Cassie for anything to add.

"Well, when you put it like that, it does sound crazy," Aletheia said.

More graphics and images came up showing fast and slowed-down images of the identified four-footed creatures. One was able to run gracefully, pounce on people, and jump up and off ledges, whereas another was far less agile, more lumbering, but just as dangerous. They seemed smaller in the environment, but the creatures were well equipped to kill unarmed humans. The beasts would latch on to the limb or part of a person, then violently shake them with their teeth clamped laterally until there was no resistance. Cassie could see that the creatures that were once cats had more fur and rounder heads, and their eyes were large for the face and slanted at an angle. The creatures that were once dogs had more angular facial features, with dark, round eyes and a square head, and they were slightly bigger than the cats.

For one of the first times, Cassie felt mortal terror, and she and Rommel were on the same page about next steps.

"I'll uplink everything we got to the *Davis* so that they can see what we're dealing with. We should leave," Cassie said.

The lieutenant was already on comms contacting the *Davis*.

"Captain, I know it sounds crazy, but wait until you see—"

Rommel was cut off by the calm though very serious voice of Gavin, whom Cassie was really missing now.

"Alpha leader, Gavin from Charlie. We've followed the blood trails to what looks like either a locked safe room, the biggest I've ever seen, or a fortified storage unit. We breached the doors and found a lot of colonists, but not all, maybe half, and sir, ah, the majority appear to be patricians, whole families slaughtered and in various stages of, well, it looks like they were eaten or something. You should be receiving images on your PDA. I kept to the officers only, including the captain as well as the doctor, and the nurse," Gavin said.

Cassie lunged for her PDA and saw nothing. She stood up and looked at Rommel's, and the sight was monstrous—severed heads, limbs, trunks everywhere, with torn clothes and bits and pieces of both human parts too mauled to identify. A feeling of acid reflux seemed to explode in Cassie's mouth, and she inadvertently held on to Rommel's shoulder for support.

"What the hell," Aletheia said. *"It looks like a feeding pit."*

"Alpha leader? Sorry to bother, but I got an evolving sitrep—the doctor and nurse insist on investigating the scene.

I am standing guard in the room, and I relocated the squad to choke points for our back door. The perimeter is secure for you to bring Cassandra for review," Gavin said.

Cassie and Rommel shared a moment of confusion together.

"Why should I bring her there? It sounds like the action's done, and you have the areas locked down," Rommel asked.

"Well, sir, let me show you," Gavin said. Moving up to the back wall with his PDA video, letters became clear, scrawled in what looked like blood: *Cassandra? Kurtz.*

"Well, that's foreboding. I think we should leave. Suddenly, marriage to lipless here is looking better all the time," Aletheia said.

"I agree," Cassie said quietly.

"Captain, I don't think this is a good idea," Rommel started.

The captain cut him off.

"Get down there, have the doctor confirm all the patricians there are dead, obtain DNA samples, and get a picture of you and your wife-to-be looking meaningfully at the scene. This will speed up the process in probate and might even be available by the time we get back to Earth. Got it?"

Rommel did not seem either shocked or surprised at the captain's response.

"Yes, sir. On the way, sir," he said.

Cassie shook her head in disbelief and was walking away when she saw the image showing the regent's slumped body on the desk, just the way she had found him. The computer was never turned off because "resting his eyes" meant he was gone.

CHAPTER NINETEEN

Cassie walked just ahead of Rommel and his three personal guards. There were twists and turns down darkened halls with minimal light, though enough to step around or over debris. The smell of feces, human body odor, and some other animal smells—likely from the "pets" running loose—was pervasive. A slip in blood here, and near trip there, the travel to the location was fraught with pitfalls and stumbling blocks, from broken chairs, strollers, and tables to desks, paper, and food. She remained alert—checking corners before moving ahead, carefully listening to the guard dictating turns and distances—while also trying to eavesdrop on the lieutenant's discussion with the captain, which moved from tense dialogue to short, cryptic answers. The only thing she clearly heard that made her want to stop listening was the captain's statement that "niggers bring money, but nigger-lovers don't." She interpreted that as meaning Lieutenant Thomas's days were numbered, and because slaves were treated as property, that might mean they would not die—today, at least.

It was an easy forty-minute, fast-paced walk, but by the time they got to Gavin's location, she was exhausted from the hypervigilance, the stress of what the captain was planning, and of course, people-eating dogs and cats.

Aletheia was unusually quiet, probably allowing her not to be distracted and focus on survival.

Cassie was surprised to find that Gavin's men had been replaced by Lieutenant Richard and his guards at the outer perimeter, and more of Rommel's guards stood at a half-open, heavily plated door. This door was different because it opened from top to bottom; it was only seven feet wide, and once closed, thick observation windows allowed for the entire room to be observed from a safe distance.

"The entrance is too small for equipment but perfect for moving crowds clustered in groups, like families," Aletheia commented.

Cassie bent down to see that the doctor and Nurse Abigal were at the far end of the room, among a sea of body parts. The scene was that of a massacre, and how they were doing their job in a red room of death was hard to imagine. While the areas outside the room and the entire base were devoid of bodies, it seemed clear to Cassie that they had all been collected and placed there.

Cassie could see that Gavin was right next to the door, just inside. She was about to crawl in through the nearly closed door when Rommel told her to stop and wait for an update. Rather than keeping vigilant on their immediate space, all the men were transfixed on the available PDAs. Suddenly, her own PDA was chiming, indicating a change. She struggled to get it out, then had to reorient the screen. Her face was heating up, and her fingertips felt slippery. Cassie stared at the device, which showed a schematic of what looked to be tunnels under their feet.

"Cassie, pull back the view to see where we are and what's happening," Aletheia said. Her AI was curt, bordering on either assertiveness or panic.

Cassie did as she was told. The larger view made far more sense of the small part she was seeing. There were four tunnels that ran underneath the station; they came from far outside New Georgia and from below the surface. The point of view provided by the geo-synchronicity of the *Davis*'s bouncing signal allowed the PDAs to see that not only did the tunnels come from generally the same direction from outside, but they also switched back and forth at times; they were four feet wide, four feet tall, and dropped at an incline of 12 to 17 percent. Without precise landmarks, it was difficult to see where the openings were, except for the one that blinked with three blips inside the room and eight blinking blips right next to it.

Farther away were three red blips moving quickly through those tunnels, entering New Georgia's perimeter and closing in fast. Based on location, it would take the blips less than a minute to get to right where she was standing.

"The opening is somewhere in the room with the doctor, and we're on the other side. That cryptic message about the doctor must mean . . . ," Aletheia said, but the rest of it was blocked out by sirens blaring and red lights pulsating in the room Cassie was in and the other, bathing both with a bloodred hue.

Cassie felt a firm hand pulling her away from the closing door. It was shutting fast, too fast for the occupants to get out from the far end of the room but an easy drop-and-roll move for Gavin. She heard the doctor and Abigal call out in shock and imagined them running for dear life.

There was no time to think. It was a raw gut feeling, an instinct that felt gritty but right. Her muscles burst with energy, and she found herself breaking the grip of whoever was pulling her away and covering the mere feet she had to traverse to the closing door. She dived under it and rolled away just in time—a second later, and she would have been trapped on the other side with Rommel, and most likely safety, or under the door where her head and limbs would have been crushed underneath.

The momentum of the dive-and-roll move landed her several inches from the door on her back. She immediately covered her eyes with her hands, one of which was clutching the PDA, showing the three red blips still coming. She didn't move at all, still as she had ever been and grief-stricken.

"I'm sorry, Aletheia. I don't know what I was thinking," Cassie said. Her eyes filled with tears, but still, the image of Aletheia came to life on her optic nerve, and in her defiant way, hands on her hips and a smile on her face, she didn't seem fazed by their impending death.

"Fuck them and their plans. We go out on our own terms. I would rather die on my feet with you and good people than live on my knees with scum like Rommel and Bennett," Aletheia said.

As if on cue, she opened her eyes and saw Gavin bending over her, offering her his hand to get up. The doctor and Abigal were almost on top of her by the time she stood up.

"Gavin? Why didn't you get out? You were right there! You could have made it out with Rommel's team," Cassie said.

"Yup. I didn't want the doctor and nurse to be alone. When they moved my squad out, I stayed behind. I figured they were going to do something like this. I hate it when I'm right," he said.

Without another word, he pulled his sidearm and three ammo

clips out, then handed them to her. Abigal looked sick and scared. The doctor, heaving from the sprint and anger, was catching his breath.

Cassie held out the PDA with her left hand; the graphics showed that the red dots were closing fast on their location. In her right hand was the sidearm, outstretched in the direction the dots were approaching. Gavin mirrored the movement. The siren cut off, and the alarm light stopped strobing, but it remained infrared in color. Cassie was grateful to some degree because it hid the grotesque image of bodies ripped apart by whatever was heading toward them. The smell wasn't as bad as she thought, and she briefly wondered if there were industrial fans somewhere.

"Any intel on what's coming?" Gavin asked.

"Large mutant cats and dogs. Really big ones with massive jaws, fangs, and claws, I'd guess, to have done all of this," Cassie said.

"Well, that explains the blood spatters and dismemberment. It also looks like the bodies were herded into piles," the doctor added.

Lieutenant Thomas was standing erect with his primary weapon already in his hands, and Nurse Abigal was holding his sidearm with two hands. The doctor took a quick look, swiftly shouldered his rifle, corrected her gun grip and orientation, pointed it away from hitting any of them, and switched the safety off.

"Anything that moves that isn't us, shoot. Once your twenty rounds are done, stay behind me or Gavin, no matter what," she heard the doctor say.

"I enjoyed working with you, Doctor," Gavin said, eyes locked down on range, searching for a target.

"Me too. Sorry you both got caught up here," the doctor said. Cassie interpreted that he was referring to her and Abigal.

Cassie switched her focus to the dwindling distance the red blips were covering. Cassie had a lot to say, things she had wished she had done and said. It galled her that they were going to kill the doctor just for being, well, a stand-up guy. It still galled her that Rommel and Bennett would live to spread lies about her and the others. But she focused on the threat. If there were three, maybe this improvised fire team could survive in part. Maybe.

"Two hundred feet," Cassie said.

"Hey, Nurse, I gave you a name instead of that awful number you're called. I call you 'Abigal' and the other nurse 'Nancy.' I just wanted you to know," Cassie added.

Abigal broke her intent gaze from down range and was at first perplexed, and then it seemed to make sense.

"Nice name. I like it," she said.

"Good. I call you 'Gavin' because that's what you told me," Cassie said, turning to her former night-shift guard.

Not flinching a bit, slowly scanning the target areas with precision, Gavin gave her a one-word response: "Interesting."

"One hundred fifty feet," Cassie said.

"What's my name?" the doctor asked.

If the situation wasn't so dire, the chuckles might have been enjoyable.

"Sorry, Doc, but you kept your name like Gavin. If you had a number as a name, I might have called you Rene," Cassie said.

The room was motionless. Breathing and some low-volume chatter coming from the doctor's headset were the only sounds breaking the eerie calm.

"One hundred feet," Cassie announced. She could feel her

heart racing, sweat dripping on her cheeks; her scalp and hair were wet.

More time. More chatter from the mic and their own breathing.

"Fifty feet," Cassie said.

"I love you. You are my best friend," Aletheia said. She briefly appeared and dropped out of sight so as not to distract Cassie from what was coming next.

"I love you, too, Aletheia," Cassie said.

The room remained still. Cassie looked down range and saw nothing. She looked at her screen and saw that the three blips had rapidly decelerated and were just below them. There was no movement from the blips and a distinct lack of the wild animal sounds she expected to hear.

The three dots started to move slowly toward them, but the graphic gave the impression that they were still underfoot, not aboveground. The motion seemed to stop just under them and then, mysteriously, accelerated away from their location, and then they were off-screen. Cassie pulled the view back to show Rommel and all his dots on the other side of the door. She looked up and saw outlines of men looking down at their own screens. She looked back down and saw that the three red blips had once again slowed to a stop. Then, the graphic showed them moving upward.

Cassie shook the screen to make sure it was nothing mechanical.

"What's wrong?" the doctor asked.

"I have no breach, no movement, and no targets," Gavin said.

Cassie took another second to confirm she was reading it right.

"Fuck me," Cassie said.

"You said it, sister," Aletheia chimed in.

"Talk to me. Where are they?" Gavin asked. For a man about to die, he was cool about it.

Cassie reoriented the screen in the opposite direction from the original view and was now facing the door that Rommel and his men were standing behind. All sets of eyes clustered around her PDA to see for themselves.

"Those blips are on the other side. They passed by us," she said.

All eyes looked up to the safety glass and immediately saw bursts of firearms and flashes of light, and then there were blood spatters hitting the windows, as if pints of paint were being hurled at it. The cries, panic, and shouting of orders from the other side of the door were punctuated by gunfire, all coming over the doctor's headpiece still hanging on his utility belt.

Cassie was transfixed by the shadows, brief images, and then blood and more movement beyond the door, all happening within seconds that dragged on forever. The cacophony of sounds and voices rapidly dwindled until there was nothing to be heard other than the captain's voice demanding an update and animalistic growls hinting at monsters just feet away. But it was the screams that really struck her. The high-pitched screams of pain and fright that suddenly stopped made her feel uneasy. The thought that she could have been the victim, and still might be, chilled her to the bone.

Cassie took a step to look through the windows to confirm what she surmised must have happened. Gavin pulled her back gently.

"If those things see you or sense motion, they might come

looking for us. Hey, Doc, kill your headset. Everyone, turn off your lights, anything that hums or makes a noise, and be quiet," Gavin instructed.

Cassie followed Gavin's direction and saw that her PDA still registered three red blips on the other side of the door, their own four white blips, and now two blue blips, mere feet from them. Her breath came up short; a quick intake of air, and she held her breath, closed and reopened her eyes to make sure she was right.

"What do you got?" Gavin said.

Cassie whispered. She had no idea if it made any sense, but she did anyway.

"Two blue blips behind us. Five feet, maybe. No movement. Just there," Cassie said.

There was a delay of a fraction of a second in Gavin's response.

"Blue, you said? Not red?" Gavin asked.

"Yes," she said.

Cassie saw Gavin nodding, as if he knew something.

"All right, everyone: keep your fingers off the triggers and point your weapons down so no friendly fire. I'll take the shots if it comes to that. From three," Gavin said.

Cassie took a deep breath.

"I'm sure he knows what he's doing," Aletheia said for reassurance.

"Three . . . two . . . one . . . NOW!"

PART VII

"One person's dystopia is another's paradise,"
Aletheia said.

CHAPTER TWENTY

"Well, this is, well, unexpected," Aletheia said.

Cassie's initial line of sight was above the two blue blips that were captured on her screen. She dropped her gaze, and she was immediately struck by their dark features, with one having white skin and the other brown. Both had long hair, but the young man's hair was perfectly spherical, puffy, like a fully filled black paintbrush, and the young woman's hair was the darkest she'd ever seen; it flowed beyond her pale shoulders. Both were naked, with different straps and belts holding various things, but most conspicuous were their weapons, edge weapons at various lengths, and each shouldered an old-style semiautomatic rifle with clips expertly placed along their midline for fast deployment.

While it was easy to see they were in their midteens, three things jumped out to Cassie: they were not ashamed about their bodies; they seemed comfortable in a room filled with pieces of humans all around with four armed strangers staring at them; and the only blemishes visible were on their knees, elbows, and feet, as if they were traversing rocks and sand.

The teens remained silent, just observing them and making no movements, as if to not startle the adults. While they looked, well, primitive, without clothes, coverings, and up-to-date equipment, their silence felt uncomfortable, foreign, as if part of a tribe not familiar with her own.

"Do you think they understand us?" Abigal asked.

"Developmentally, they should, though their language might be different or underdeveloped," the doctor said.

"I'm more curious about how they snuck up on us without a sound," Gavin said.

Gavin kept his sights on them as he spoke. Abigal looked at them as if she was doing a visual inspection. The doctor took the initiative by taking a slow step forward, letting his rifle fall gently beside him and raising his hands in surrender.

"We are not going to hurt you. We are peaceful. We mean you no harm," he said.

The choice of words, carefully and slowly spoken, clarified their threat level, their peaceful intentions, and that they were not a danger. The doctor wanted to be clear that they were safe.

The two young people looked at him and the rest carefully, then at each other and back to them again.

"Are you for real?" the young man asked. His tone clearly indicated he was annoyed.

"Really? You think we're Martians or something?" the young woman chimed in. The sarcasm was unmistakable.

"Fucking white devil," the young man said.

"What balls," she added.

Their expressions clearly revealed they were older adolescents, teenagers, notorious for sarcasm, moments of brilliance, and impulsive and risky behaviors.

"What the hell is this?" Cassie said.

The young man turned to walk to the back of the wall while the girl turned and waved to them to follow.

"We got to move before the dogs and cat get our scent," she said.

Initially frozen, Cassie looked at Gavin as if looking for permission. He slowly lowered his weapon and moved in their direction.

"Makes sense what the kids are saying," he said.

Cassie did her best not to slip or step on body parts in the dim light but was trying to keep pace with the teenagers as they moved toward the far wall from the door. Even though the teens clearly understood them, the doctor conveyed his plan.

"I think I'll keep a low profile with these youths. It was stupid to assume they wouldn't understand me," the doctor said to the nurse.

"I'm embarrassed, but I thought the same thing. It looks like there's more to them than we thought," she said.

The new arrivals dodged the dismembered limbs, and once they got to the far wall, they both wiped their feet on some cleaner surfaces.

"Ugh, gross," the young woman said.

The young man moved what looked like sheets of storage cardboard and light wood and revealed the tunnel entrance from which Cassie was sure the monsters were going to emerge and kill them just minutes ago. And now they were going down that same hole.

The young man went down the hole feetfirst, on his butt and supported by his hands. The young woman got into position to do the same but obviously saw hesitation in the group.

"Here's the deal: come with us and you'll live, or stay here and be killed by those feral things or more of those 'nice' men who put you in here to die," she said.

And like that, she was out of sight, down the hole.

Everyone in the group looked at each other.

"Lieutenant? Your orders?" Gavin said.

"Are you kidding? You make the call. I have no idea what I'm doing. Assume tactical command," the doctor said.

"Smart move," Aletheia said. *"We might live to see another hour today."*

"OK. I'm point, Cassandra, Nurse, and then Doc. Shoulder weapons and move quietly. See anything odd, call it out," Gavin said.

Gavin did not wait for an answer and was already heading feetfirst down the hole.

"Yeah, nothing bad is likely to happen here," Cassie said.

There was no response as she moved quickly, feetfirst, down an incline. It was not terribly steep, but it was far from level. Sliding some, stopping, changing positions to crawl when possible, and then back again for more sliding. It was not an easy feat for her or anyone. She had no idea how the men were doing it, especially Gavin, who was more width than height. Cassie could smell dust and dirt and felt the compactness of flat stones, or maybe it was Martian clay that was not as jagged as she had originally thought.

At some point, she saw Gavin had taken a slight left into a smaller tunnel where there was a fork that offered a larger tunnel to traverse instead.

"Hey, why can't we take the larger tunnel? It'd be easier to go through. Does it go to the same place?" Cassie asked.

Gavin was now in the smaller tunnel, and she imagined that it had to be hard for him to talk and move in the tight space.

"The kids say the bigger tunnels are for our four-footed friends; they lead to and from colonies. The smaller ones are for us, since they can't fit, and they say the creatures don't bother with the small ones when the larger ones lead to more food. And I guess those creatures don't like where we're heading to, which sounds ominous," Gavin added.

The tunnel entrance was tighter, but then the space eased up a bit. It was dark except for a very faint glow stick that was jiggling far ahead, as if it was on one of the teens as a guiding light.

After what seemed like an hour, the tunnel opened enough to allow for standing in a hunched-over stance. The ground was more level, and Cassie was able to move faster. She found that she was getting tired, and she couldn't tell if it was the aftermath of a near-death experience, an adrenaline dump, or the hard work to move quickly in a completely dark tunnel, which was more spacious than before, but not by much.

Either Gavin was able to read minds, or he was experiencing the same fatigue she was sure everyone was feeling.

"Three-minute break?" she heard him ask. An unintelligible response came back, and movement ahead finally stopped.

"Two-minute break. Take my water and send it down the line, and when the next break happens, send it back up, and so forth. Pass it along," Gavin said.

As instructed, Cassie savored the sip of water, passed it along, and sat down. It was the longest calm moment she'd had that day. Sitting in total darkness, no sounds to be heard but other people breathing and fidgeting, was almost peaceful. Short-lived, but a moment of quiet.

"We're putting a lot of faith in two naked kids," Cassie muttered.

She really didn't think she was going to get a response, so she was surprised by Gavin's answer.

"They have the advantage. They've obviously been here longer, know things about the creatures we dodged and these tunnels, seemed to know when to show up, and we had few options. Less about faith and more about intel, poor options versus being dead faster."

Cassie thought about it. What else could she have done? The creatures were right next door when they left and hopefully feasting for a while, with more guards farther away from them to attack. Hiding didn't work, but going in the opposite direction did seem to be a smart play.

Movement picked up ahead of her, and Gavin called back.

"We're on the move. Pass along," he said.

More small tunnel entrances led to more dark, winding tunnels. More dirt, dust, heat, and human smells due to exertion. The travel variations ranged from crawling to hunching over to crawling again, with the tunnel entrances remaining consistently small enough for only people to get through. Cassie counted eight times that they stopped, rested for two minutes, and then started to move again. Cassie assumed the rests were permitted since the creatures were not able to pursue them in the tight tunnels. She still held the fear that the monsters could be tracking them anyway, and she wondered how they would be able to move faster if they had to, especially with her labored breathing and careful pacing. And how there was still oxygen, presumably under the Martian surface, was a mystery to her.

The tunnel had expanded again in width but barely in height, and it was slowly but noticeably getting warmer with every step. It was also evident they were still going deeper into the planet's crust.

Then, when Cassie was feeling on the verge of wanting to

die on the ninth break, a glimmer of hope arrived. There was a light ahead, very dim, and more likely still far ahead, but it was definitely an opening.

"Finally," Aletheia said. It startled Cassie because she'd been quiet so long; it was almost as if she'd forgotten that Aletheia was her permanent resident.

The movement ahead slowed to a stop, fortunately.

"Break. Getting toward the end, where we can walk upright and possibly set up camp and rest? Hang tight. Pass along," Gavin said.

Cassie did what she was told. The fatigue and aches all over her body were complete, but when there's hope, the impossible becomes achievable.

"Once more into the breach," Aletheia said.

"Once more," Cassie started, but she was too tired to finish. No one asked her what she said. She was grateful not to have to explain.

CHAPTER TWENTY ONE

"We were only in those tunnels for a couple of hours—how is it possible that I'm so exhausted?" Cassie said.

About a thousand feet from the exit, Cassie, her team, and the two adolescents were standing fully erect, bending and stretching as much as they could. Between the crawling and sliding in a confined space, most of the time at a declining angle; the total absence of light except for the glow stick ahead; and the cramped, slow movement in dust, sweat, and body odor, anyone on two feet would be stressed and pained. And throughout their journey, it had been getting increasingly warm; now, near the end of the tunnel, it was significantly hotter. At least there was more height and width, expansive in comparison to what they'd endured; there was room for single-file upright progression and little chance of bumping your head, which felt like a luxury. It was so hot, Cassie was dying to shed her clothes. This heat contributed to the mounting list of barriers.

The doctor suggested lying flat on the ground for five minutes to realign and support the spine, which the young people complained about. They simply sat it out while Cassie, the doctor, and Abigal complied, lying head to foot in a row.

Gavin remained standing, leaning on the wall, stretching but vigilant.

"He's always on alert, isn't he?" Aletheia said.

"Yup. Good thing too. I'm not sure we would've made it without him," Cassie said.

"Shit," Aletheia said.

It took a mere second for Cassie to realize that she responded to Aletheia as if she were alone. She closed her eyes, waiting for the questions about what she'd just said and why. Instead, she got another surprise.

"So is your AI encapsulated near the cerebellum, or did they position it in an entirely different place?" Abigal asked.

At first, Cassie couldn't believe what she'd heard. Abigal's question was casual, as if Aletheia was well known to the group. The nurse wasn't even looking at her when she asked. No one chimed in to ask what she was talking about.

Cassie lifted her head and glanced at the doctor; it looked like he'd fallen asleep. Gavin just nodded and continued scanning the room. She couldn't see the two teenagers, but they hadn't piped up. Cassie lowered her head, eyes narrowed, and then she finally spoke.

"How long have you all known?" she asked.

The silence seemed like everyone was taking a moment to recall when they first figured it out.

"Pleb 92—or what did you call her? It's a much better name," Abigal said.

"Nancy," Cassie said.

"Right, that's a nice name. Well, Nancy told me how you figured out the location and code for breaching the locks back on the ship," Abigal explained.

"Nancy told me the same thing," the doctor added, "and

apparently, the captain thought of it, too, so he increased surveillance, and I reviewed your chart. I guessed that charge you got had to have been something to revive your AI, like electroshock for the heart, but I've never seen anything like that before."

Cassie felt embarrassed, thinking that she had kept everyone in the dark with her ace up her sleeve, only to find out everyone knew about Aletheia.

She looked over at Gavin, who continued scanning even as he listed off his clues. "The nurse told me how you breached all systems to help the slaves, and then you answered all the verbal challenges at the security doors without a problem, and I heard you talking to yourself or clearing your throat a couple of times as if answering a question. Plus, you said the name 'Aletheia,' so I figured that was your AI implant we all heard about in your hearing way back."

Cassie sat up from her prone position, dumbfounded. She was even more embarrassed by the attention to detail, with Gavin referencing her hearing closing from more than three years ago.

"OK, Cassie, tell them from me to them, 'You all suck,'" Aletheia said.

"Agreed. Aletheia says, 'You all suck.'"

The laugh was brief but full-fledged and heartfelt. Cassie would have lain back down and just slept, but the naked teens clearly wanted to continue the trek, as if they had something else better to do.

"Hey, we've got to move. After we get out of here, we've got a long journey ahead," the young woman said.

"It's not going to be easy, so less talk, more walk," her male counterpart said.

Cassie and the others got up and prepared to move out.

Gavin took point and made the comment, "Kids' got leadership skills."

"They just need to tweak the motivational pieces," the doctor added.

Up on her feet, Cassie was again on the move.

CHAPTER TWENTY TWO

The "light" up ahead was relative to what Cassie had experienced in the tunnels; the enormous cave was still dark, with red and midnight-blue hues that provided enough light for shadows from objects, but their outlines were subtle. Gavin and the two teens were in shadow, barely visible to the human eye even when two to three feet away. There was less dust and body odor but more of an acid and ash smell. The heat and low rumbling continued, and except for being able to walk erect, there was little comfort in the current conditions. Cassie was opening and closing her eyes to adjust to the change in temperature and to make sure she wasn't hallucinating. She was shocked and confused by the hellscape in front of her. She felt more than saw the doctor and nurse come up behind her.

"Holy shit," the doctor said.

The vista overlooking the scene was as impressive as it was expansive. If there was a ceiling to the cavern, it was too high and dark to see. If it wasn't for the massive stalagmites hanging above them, she would have thought they were outside. The landscape itself, several hundred feet down, was dramatic, with a river of molten lava snaking far to the horizon, black areas of what looked like plants abutting large lakes of what looked like water. The lava flow did provide illumination that was glowing red, but Cassie still felt she would need time for her eyes to get used to the darkness. And then there was the fact they were breathing outside the constructed colony, just as they had been while they were in the tunnels all that time.

"How is this all possible? Maybe permafrost from above? Electrostatic discharge separating water molecules into vapor and air?" the nurse said.

"Yeah. Add lava, heat, and whatever those stalagmites are holding, and it's a real primeval soup for life we've got going," the doctor said.

Everyone was quiet until the doctor spoke again.

"You know, Walter, the *Davis*'s engineer, was talking about how the terraforming installations had become inefficient over the last thirty years. I wonder if the nanites not only built the processors on the surface, but maybe wherever they found open spaces like this, underground and otherwise, they did the same thing," the doctor said.

"All possible," Aletheia said. *"Probably more complicated than that. It always is,"* she added.

Cassie was pulled out of her thoughts by the teens. She watched them head in two different directions behind two separate large rocks beside the tunnel cave exit, move some unseen covers, and produce two large bags. Presumably, the teens had hidden the bags before meeting them. Something in the young woman's bag was moving. She noticed and made a face.

"Jacob? What the fuck? I thought you killed all the bugs. If it laid eggs in this, I will mess you up," she said.

The young man didn't respond but continued with his own bag, then moved to another part of the tunnel exit, presumably where there were more bags.

The young woman rummaged around in her bag and took out what looked like a giant bug with moving legs and pincers. It was the size of two large, closed fists. Without hesitation and with expert precision, she firmly gripped the creature by the neck, avoiding the sharp mandibles, and shoved a double-edged knife through its head.

The doctor and nurse looked on with pure professional curiosity and enthusiasm. Gavin similarly observed, but his focus was clearly different.

"Those things might be good protein sources, and that water could be drinkable. With plant life and heat available, this place might be habitable," Gavin said.

"Those are a lot of 'ifs,' but I guess we'll find out. No one is interested in going back up, are they?" the doctor said.

No one responded. Cassie assumed there was tacit agreement.

"One person's dystopia is another's paradise," Aletheia said.

Cassie nodded in agreement, then turned to the young woman.

"What is that thing?" Cassie asked.

She had seen old visuals of sea creatures, lobsters, and crabs, and she thought they looked a lot like what the girl was holding.

"Lunch in ten. Hey, Jacob, be useful and get a fire going for bugs and water. I'm starving," she said.

Cassie made a move to ask more questions, which clearly annoyed the young woman, who was still holding the massive dead insectoid in her hand. It was obvious that anything or anyone getting in the way of food and eating would be a problem.

"Ah, so he's Jacob—and you?"

"Yeah, thanks for asking. We've got names. I'm Sarah and that's Jacob. You're welcome for saving your life, and we have, like, days to get home, so can we get a move on?" Sarah said.

"Wow! She reminds me of your older sister. What a sarcastic—" Aletheia said.

Cassie put her hands up, hoping to stop the situation from escalating.

"I'm sorry, Sarah. We were too rushed and stressed at the surface and in the tunnels to ask questions like your names, and this is the first time in hours I've felt safe—and in this environment," Cassie said as she gestured at their primordial soup of a landscape, "that's saying a lot."

The teen seemed to get what Cassie was saying. Sarah's initial expression of annoyance had shifted from questioning why she was being interrupted to why someone might be confused in such a strange environment, an environment that she must have been used to but new arrivals found incredibly strange.

"And I'm just confused. Why did you help us, and why did you bring us here? You and Jacob got us out of some deep shit. We're just confused and out of our depth. I mean, look at this," Cassie said, waving her arms all around her again. "We're all used to recycled air, controlled environments, and pressurized living spaces. Now, here we are in an open environment with extreme elements and, well, massive bugs for food. You can see how this is all difficult to process."

The plea seemed to have the desired effect. Sarah took a moment to organize her thoughts and then spoke.

"Jacob and I were sent to find you and bring you and the others back home," she started.

"Others?" Abigal said.

"Yup. Anyone who was *not* the white, blue-eyed devil," Sarah said.

It wasn't lost on the doctor that he was the subject of contention.

"OK. It's good to know your role," the doctor commented.

"The only reason he's alive is because we saw him trying to protect her," Sarah said, pointing to Abigal, "and the other white devils clearly cast him out of their clan."

"The enemy of my enemy—" Gavin started but was cut off by Sarah.

"Is my brother. That's why we save you and others like you," Sarah said.

"OK," Cassie said. She hoped further information was coming.

"Our home is far away from these tunnels. We use the tunnels to free others, and if they want to come, they can. The dogs and cats burrow for food, and we tunnel to raid the camps on the surface."

"All right. Why me?" Cassie asked.

"Well, we saw you years ago on news feeds, and you said, 'Good luck, Kurtz.' You were in the old book, one of the ones we read. The elders said we needed you, so they devised a plan to get you here, and here you are," Sarah said.

"A book?" the doctor asked.

*"Fuck me—*Heart of Darkness*,"* Aletheia said.

"*Heart of Darkness*. You have a copy of *Heart of Darkness*, with the character Mr. Kurtz, or Colonel Kurtz, right?" Cassie said.

Cassie was deep in thought, and the others were quietly trying to fully grasp what was happening.

"Hey, Sarah? Looks like Nellie and Rob left here two hours ago. It looks like they saved some others too. They say they have five Black women and a white woman with black hair who says she's a nurse," Jacob said.

Cassie's heart fluttered. More of her friends didn't die. If Jacob was telling the truth, Lucia and the others were free.

"Oh, wow! That's great," Aletheia said.

"Crap," Sarah said. Her shoulders slumped, and she looked disappointed. She looked at Cassie, and her pouty expression conveyed her displeasure.

"So I'm guessing you'd like to hurry and catch up with them," she said.

Cassie looked at her team. They were obviously willing to move out and catch up. The fatigue she was experiencing and the journey to date had taken a toll on her, and she had to guess for the others as well. Cassie was anxious to catch up and make sure the others were all right but then thought twice.

"If we rest and eat now, will we be able to catch up with them later?" Cassie asked.

Sarah's demeanor and attitude totally shifted from dour and depressed to smiles and enthusiasm.

"You bet! Jacob, get the fire going and start boiling the water; we finally get to eat and sleep for a bit. Fuck yeah!" Sarah said.

"And those creatures won't come down here at the smell of food and eat us?" Gavin asked.

"Nope. The tunnels we came in through are too tight, and they hate the smell down here," Jacob answered.

Cassie was surprised by how quickly the teens' attitudes changed. The joy brought by the prospect of rest, food, and water was universal.

Cassie moved closer to the edge of the plateau to look at the primitive landscape. A river of molten rock, a black abyss of darkness, and life—plants, water, wild and carnivorous mammals, and bugs—all awaiting them within the dark shadows of a black continent.

Gavin came up beside her and said, "Good call."

"I'm glad Nancy and the others are alive," the doctor said.

"Me too. I can't wait to hear about what happened to them," Abigal said.

All four stood beside each other and looked out quietly over the primordial soup, which, for all intents and purposes, was their new home. It had been mere hours since landfall and where they were now, but a lot had changed.

"Well, this looks ominous. But still, it's kind of exciting. I mean, we should have died a while ago, but here we are. What do you think is out there?" Aletheia said.

"I wish I knew what was out there, but I bet we're all going to find out," Cassie said.

"If tomorrow is anything like today, we're going to be busy," Gavin said.

"Yup. We sure will," Aletheia said.

EPILOGUE

"Terminate her command with extreme prejudice," the older judge said.

"Magistrate, it's been four years since New Georgia fell. And I have not been anywhere near Mars to be held responsible for the two other colonies going dark. Maybe they are rebelling," said Willard Bennett, former captain of the *Jefferson Davis*.

The room itself was too large for eight people—three judges elevated above where a prisoner would stand and four armed guards, two flanking each side of Bennett's back, close enough to grab him but far enough to respond if attacked. Dim lighting, dark wood-like material absorbing the low light, no chairs but for the judges, and no spectator benches. He was sure the minimal lighting over the judges was to cast shadows, obscure expressions, and create mystery. This courtroom was for closed-session, high-security meetings. Bennett had been there before his last tour as captain of the *Jefferson Davis*, where his instructions were clear and to the point. He had come to understand that if he had followed orders and simply killed the prisoner he was transporting and made it look like an accident, he might have kept his commission, status, and ship. It took him six months of solitary confinement to come to that decision. Greed and the opportunity to be rich ruined him and killed his command staff. Hard lessons. It took an additional six months in the general prison population to own his role in his present situation, but he was not going to be held accountable for events occurring while he was en route back from Mars and in prison.

Honestly, how can it be all my fault what happened to them after? he thought.

"Not completely true. Your decision to disregard the original directives given to you in this very room may have set the stage for what happened," the older of the three military judges said.

Bennett was still standing, as was customary for a military prisoner in front of a review panel. In front of him was a table with three monitors showing security footage feeds from different locations of patricians being attacked, eviscerated, and dismembered by large dog- and catlike creatures. Other images showed half-dressed primitives carefully, methodically, and covertly breaking into storage and munitions stockades at various secured colonies, ushering slaves and plebs and anyone else along with them. He had seen these images before over the years and had come to hate them, especially the ones that showed his former chief medical officer tending to Black slaves, and even more, he hated a relatively small, athletic woman with red hair leading the raids, whom he once knew as Cassandra.

"Are you paying attention, convict?" another judge asked.

"Yes," Bennett said.

He was still not used to being spoken down to or his words being challenged. He had been interrupted, reprimanded, and put in isolation for disagreeing with any decisions these younger judges made. He continued to practice restraint. The bright-orange jumpsuit and limb- and throat-locking devices truly added to his fall from grace, with his uniform, property, riches, power, and position stripped upon his return to Earth two years ago. He was far thinner now, and he had to harden up and remember all the military fighting, training, and exercises he never thought he would actually have to use once he commanded his ship. In his time in prison, he'd had to live with slaves, plebs, and lesser humans. The poor food, lack of warm clothes and bedding, threats and acts of violence all the time, and no privacy anywhere—all of this was hell to him. He had been ill more times now than he had been in his life, and since his annual genetic dosages were no longer available to him, he would age and be susceptible to cancer, a disease effectively cured by patrician science for those patricians *in good standing*, which he was not. Still, it was being talked down to that bothered him the most.

"If you had managed your prisoner well, your command staff and guards might have lived. And if you had taken the time to launch a thorough investigation and destroyed those monsters and stopped those mutineers who assisted this Cassandra Kurtz, New Alabama and Mason Dixon might still be running, and New Georgia could have been rebuilt."

"I mean, if you had just killed that girl as originally ordered instead of being greedy, you might not be where you are," another judge added.

That statement hurt the most. *There is nothing worse than someone else pointing out a personal, massive mistake that can't be defended or denied,* Bennett thought. Not a day went by when he had not recounted the errors and lack of judgment. Maybe this was the curse of imprisonment, to review all you did wrong and how it would have been simpler to stay on mission. Dumb.

The older judge continued as if he had not been interrupted at all.

"Now, I don't know if it was incompetence or poor judgment and you hoped all of this was going to blow over, but you have a chance to offset your failure and make things right."

Bennett looked up from the monitors, which were still displaying havoc, chaos, well-orchestrated raids, and a familiar face—Gavin, he remembered, whose image was now captured on security cameras. This betrayal had made his heart jump, but hearing that he could somehow make his situation better caused him more dread than excitement.

He was afraid to talk, so he waited. It had taken him years to learn not to speak and wait for his "betters" to talk first.

"You left a total mess on Mars. We have no idea where this Cassandra Kurtz is and where she is getting her people, but it is evident that she is behind all these attacks that challenge the very foundation of our society and jeopardize our expansion on Mars. She has evaded, escaped, and at times destroyed any unified force against her, and after nearly four years of being unchecked, we must put an end to her," the older judge said.

"Yes, sir," Bennett said. He really had no idea where this was going. He had already lost everything, so he could at least listen.

"Officer," one of the judges said. "Play the transmissions we picked up from these terrorists."

Bennett had no idea what the judge was talking about. There was a blanket of silence until it was broken by a woman's voice, subdued anger behind the thoughts that were thought out and direct, leaving no mystery as to who she was, what she wanted, and who the enemy was. Everything had been visual up until that point, but now, in place of images the screen reflected audio waves, rising and falling with every word the woman said. Bennett sat in dissonance of the Cassandra who was on his ship and the voice that speaking now.

The low male voice documenting the radio transmission source, time, and location highlighted Cassandra Kurtz's strong, unforgiving, and confident voice. Not rushed or particularly feminine but deliberate with smooth cadence and even tone. Somehow, just the way she spoke was just as threatening, as frightening, as the message she conveyed.

Transmission frequency 145.100 Hz—New Alabama, All Citizen's Band

". . . how is that I bleed like you, eat like you, shit like you, fuck like you, and will die like you but lived a much better life than you? No disease. No sickness. No struggles. That's what it was like when I was one of them: a patrician, first citizen to stolen wealth from plebs, surfers, and slaves. All power. No accountability. I was no better than you . . . we know where you are. You are out of your element. This is our world. Can you find us? Do you dare? You lack conviction. You have no moral compass. This is why we will prevail while you fail."

Transmission frequency 412.289 Hz—Mason Dixon, Expedition team Bravo Six, forward operations—Echo-Tango 12

". . . now. I am you. I am you and we are here, living in the dark shadows of a black continent on a red planet. And above are them—our enslaved brothers and sisters. Above us, on the surface, are their slave owners. We must free the slaves and all who want to join, and we

must kill any that get in our way . . . they are no better than us . . ."

Transmission frequency 412.338 Hz—Mason Dixon, Expedition team Bravo Six, forward operations—Echo-Tango 12

". . . They are looking for us. Every step deeper into our home, they die. They're not strong. They are soft, comfortable, and weak. They started with twenty-three soldiers and now they are down to four, the four horsemen. The rest have fled the horrors that is our home. Madness killed them. Weakness killed them. The heavy weight of darkness killed them. Every passing day they look for us, they lose more of themselves to terror . . . there is nothing here for you other than sheer terror and horror."

Whether it was staged or not, the silence felt heavy, but her voice still echoed in his head; the taunting, judgment, her harsh conviction that she and the insurrectionists were far *more* while people like him, the judges, all patricians, were less than.

How the hell did this happen? What happened to her, he thought.

"This woman is a menace to our industry and expansion. She is costing us billions in lost revenue and profits, and word of her freeing the slaves and plebs has made it back here, causing more trouble on Earth. We are on the brink of an apocalypse, now, every day she lives and transmits this shit," another judge said, pointing at him as if he was personally responsible.

There was a brief silence. Bennett wanted to make sure it was his time to speak.

"Yes, sir. Where do I fit in?" he asked.

The silence was deafening. Even with the shadows obscuring their faces, he knew that all three judges were staring at him. His stomach tightened, and his mouth and throat went dry. He ran a hundred ideas of what was coming next, the most likely of which he thought would be a public execution for everything that had gone wrong.

"You are reinstated as *acting* captain of a Plebian Auxiliary Corps task force to find this Kurtz woman; locate and destroy her base of operation; end her reign of terror; stop the loss of property, especially the slaves; and execute all former *Davis* crew, regardless of position and citizen status. Do not leave a stone upon a stone, *Acting Captain* Bennett."

Bennett froze in place. He recounted each word to make sure he was not hallucinating or dreaming. He had to clear his dry throat before he spoke.

"Sorry, but, um, are you sending me back to Mars to kill Kurtz and everyone, and if so, I'll get my life back?" he asked.

"You will get a part of it back: full citizenship with medical benefits, captain rank but no ship, and you would be able to retire with an honorable discharge upon returning to Earth. Whatever property you reclaim will go to eliminating your prison term and filling your coffers, and while you will be on a short leash with the ship's captain and command crew, you'll be free from your cell. That's a pretty good deal, considering we could go with someone else," the judge said.

It is a good deal, Bennett thought. *Almost too good to be true.* Why didn't they go with someone else? He wondered if it was a real deal or whether, if he did what he was told to do and completed the operations, he would have an "accident" like what was originally planned for Cassandra. He wondered if he should pass, spend his ten years in prison, and hope he wasn't killed by the other inmates or guards. By the time he would get back to Mars, six Earth years would have passed, and his targets might be dug in deeper, with better resources and positioning. The whole planet might have changed by then. Maybe none of his kind, first-class citizens, patricians, would even be left alive by then. His eyebrows furrowed at the new thought. No more partitions on the whole planet. None.

"Well, Bennett? Are you in or out?" the older judge asked.

His moment was up. He did his best to snap to attention, as if he was fully committed to the offer.

"Yes, sirs. Search, locate, and destroy the terrorists' base; terminate Cassandra's command; locate and return all property, especially slaves; reestablish societal, political, and economic structures for the remaining colonies and rebuild the potentially lost locations; and return to Earth," Bennett said. He did his best to project authority in his prisoner's orange jumpsuit and limb and neck restraints. His response was precise, crisp, and delivered with command, just as he remembered from before his fall from grace.

"We need you to document both visually and by DNA, but preferably bring her body, or if it's easier, just bring her severed head back to be a lesson for all others who challenge our thinking to see," said the third judge, who had been silent throughout the proceedings.

"Her head, sir?" Bennett asked.

"Yes, Acting Captain. Terminate her command with extreme prejudice," the older judge said.

With a nod, Bennett agreed, and his limb and neck restraints fell right off, leaving his body feeling lighter. He felt his stomach settling and relaxing for the first time in years.

And while he felt a wave of relief, he was surprised he did not feel anger or hatred toward his targets; rather, he felt excitement. He couldn't figure out why, but he embraced the offer to be an assassin with zeal, though he was not remotely positive he would carry out *all* his stated objectives.

"Uncertainty is good," Bennett said to himself.

"What did you say, Captain?" the judge asked.

"Nothing, sir. I shall proceed," Bennett said.

The End

www.ingramcontent.com/pod-product-compliance
Lightning Source LLC
LaVergne TN
LVHW010101110826
845155LV00028B/432
9781942708537